PIG HEART BOY

malorie
blackman

CORGI BOOKS

PIG-HEART BOY
A CORGI BOOK 978 0 552 56790 9

First published in Great Britain by Doubleday,
an imprint of Random House Children's Publishers UK
A Random House Group Company

Doubleday edition published 1997
Corgi edition published 1998
Corgi edition reissued 2004

This edition published 2012

2 4 6 8 10 9 7 5 3 1

The Random House Group Limited supports The Forest Stewardship Council (FSC®),
the leading international forest certification organisation. Our books carrying the FSC
label are printed on FSC® certified paper. FSC is the only forest certification scheme
endorsed by the leading environmental organisations, including Greenpeace. Our paper
procurement policy can be found at www.randomhouse.co.uk/environment

MIX
Paper from
responsible sources
FSC® C016897
www.fsc.org

Set in Bembo

Corgi Books are published by Random House Children's Publishing UK,
61–63 Uxbridge Road, London W5 5SA

www.**randomhousechildrens**.co.uk
www.**totallyrandom**.co.uk

Addresses for companies within The Random House Group Limited can be found at:
www.randomhouse.co.uk/offices.htm

THE RANDOM HOUSE GROUP Limited Reg. No. 954009

A CIP catalogue record for this book is available from the British Library.

Printed and bound by CPI Group (UK) Ltd, Croydon, CR0 4YY

For Neil and Lizzy, with love

COVENTRY SCHOOLS' LIBRARY SERVICE

Please return this book on or before last date stamped.

r'

e

Consequences

Chapter One

Dying

I am drowning in this roaring silence.

I am drowning.

I'm going to die.

I look up through the grey-white shimmer of the swimming-pool water. High, high above I can see where the quality of the light changes. The surface. But it is metres above me. It might as well be kilometres. The chlorine stings my eyes. My lungs are on fire.

Just one breath. Just one.

I have to take a breath, even though I know that I'll be breathing in water. But my lungs are burning and my blood is roaring and my whole body is screaming out for air. If I don't take a breath, I'll burst. If I do take a breath, I'll drown. Some choice. No choice.

I close my eyes, praying hard. And kick, kick, kick. I open my eyes. The surface of the water seems even further away.

I'm going to drown.

A fact. A fact as clear, as real as the silence around me. Part of me – a tiny, tiny part of me – laughs. I am going to drown.

After everything I've been through in the last few months, this is how I'm going to bow out. One thought rises up in my mind.

One thought . . .

Alex . . .

I stop kicking. I have no energy left.

I stop fighting. I'm so tired. I can feel my body begin to sink.

Now for the hard part.

Now for the easy part.

Now for the hard part.

Give in. Let go.

Just one breath . . .

Just one . . .

Just . . .

Cause

Chapter Two

Ticking

The noise was deafening. Shouting, screaming, laughing, shrieking – it was so thunderous. I thought my head was about to explode. I took a deep breath, breathed out, inhaled again, then dipped down until my head was completely under water.

Silence.

Peace.

It was like a radio being switched off. I sat down at the bottom of the swimming pool and opened my eyes. The chlorine in the water stung, but better that than not seeing what was coming and being kicked in the face. I would've liked to stay down there for ever, but within seconds my lungs were aching and there came a sharp, stabbing pain in my chest. My blood roared like some kind of angry monster in my ears.

I closed my eyes and stood up slowly. If I had to emerge, it would be at my own pace and in my own time – no matter how much my body screamed at me to take a breath as fast as I could. I was the one in control. Not my lungs. Not my blood. Not my heart.

'Cam, are you all right?'

I opened my eyes. Marlon stood in front of me, his green eyes dark and huge with concern. I inhaled sharply, waiting for the roaring in my ears to subside. The pain in my chest took a little longer. ''Course! I'm fine,' I replied a little breathlessly.

'What were you doing?'

'Just sitting down.'

Marlon frowned. 'Is that smart?'

'I was just sitting down. Don't fuss. Sometimes you're worse than Mum and Dad,' I said.

'If your parents find out that you're here every Tuesday instead of at my house, I'm the one who'll get it in the neck – and every other bodily part,' Marlon pointed out.

I smiled. 'If you don't tell them, I won't.'

'How can you be so calm about it? Every time we come here, I'm terrified some grown-up who knows your family is going to spot you and tell your parents.' Marlon looked around the pool anxiously, as if expecting his words to come true at that precise moment.

'Marlon, you worry too much.' My smile broadened as the pain in my chest lessened.

'How long were you under water?'

'A few seconds. Why?'

'I really don't think you should . . .'

I'd had enough. 'Marlon, bog off!' I snapped. 'You're getting on my last nerve now!'

'I was just . . .'

'I know what you were doing, and you can stop it,' I said firmly. 'You're beginning to cheese me off.'

Marlon clamped his lips together tight and looked away. He was hurt and we both knew it. I fought down the urge to apologize. Why should I say I was sorry? Marlon knew how much I hated to be clucked over. But, as always, I caved in.

'Look, Marlon, I—' I got no further.

'Hey, Marlon! You on for Daredevil Dive?' Rashid called out.

'Yeah. Coming!' Marlon replied. He turned to me. 'See you in a minute.'

And with that he swam off towards the middle of the pool. I waded over to the stairs, the water sloshing around my thighs. I rubbed my eyes, which were still stinging, before climbing out. I turned to where Rashid, Nathan and Andrew were all splashing about. Marlon had just reached them. I didn't want to watch but I couldn't help it. I couldn't bring myself to look away. Instead I sat down at the edge of the pool, my legs dangling in the water as I watched my friends. I sidled a bit closer until I could hear them as well. Kicking out leisurely with my legs, I looked straight ahead, although I was listening to every word Marlon and the others said.

'Everyone ready?' asked Rashid. 'OK, let's do it. First one to dive and touch the bottom, then come back and touch the side of the pool wins. Ready . . .'

'Steady . . .'

'GO!'

In an instant all four boys disappeared under the water. I held my breath as I watched, until my lungs started to ache and my heart started to pound and I couldn't stand it any longer. And still none of my friends had emerged from the water. I gasped, my whole body screaming in angry, pained protest as I concentrated on filling my lungs.

Slow down. I've stopped holding my breath now, I told my heart. Just slow down.

I knew that within the next few weeks I'd no longer be able to come swimming with Marlon and my other friends. I knew it as surely as I knew my own name.

Because my heart was getting worse.

So I had to hang on to these last moments of independence – even if part of it was just me fooling myself. Travis, our school moron, was right about that at least. I was a weed. And a feeble one at that.

Long moments later Marlon and Andrew emerged from the water, quickly followed by Rashid, then Nathan. Some swam, some thrashed for the side of the pool. Marlon made it back first, laughing and gasping. Marlon always made it back first.

'I win! I win!' Marlon shouted.

'Let's do it again!' said Andrew. 'Only this time we have to go down and come up, then do the same again before we make for the pool side.'

I gave the water one last, vicious kick, then stood up slowly. I couldn't bear to listen to any more. It was as if there was a glass wall separating me from the rest of the world. All I could do was watch and envy my friends as they swam and dived and did whatever they wanted without a care in the world. They never bothered to ask me if I wanted to join them. They all knew I couldn't. I was weak and feeble and had to stay in the shallow end. I shouldn't have been in the pool in the first place – and we all knew it.

I turned and watched Marlon and the others play Daredevil Dive again. They were in the middle of the pool, not the deep end. The bottom of the pool sloped down gently from the shallow end for three-quarters of the pool, then came a sudden drop like the end of an underwater cliff and after that the water was really deep. That's how they played Daredevil Dive. They had to dive and touch the bottom of the pool at the deep end before emerging from the water. The deep end of the pool was several metres down so there was no way I could join in. I wondered bitterly what it must be like to kick your legs and dive down without fear that your heart would give out before you got to the bottom. What was it like to dive with a body that *could* do as your mind commanded? I would never know again.

I walked back to the changing rooms, my mind swimming as my body could not. By the entrance to the pool there was a full-length mirror. I caught sight of myself, my shoulders drooped, my mouth turned down, my eyes . . . miserable. I looked at my torso. I clenched my fist and banged it against the left side of my chest in what started off as a slow tattoo, but which grew increasingly faster and harder.

In there. I couldn't see it. But I could hear it. And feel it. And it was ruining my life. I couldn't do anything. I couldn't run, I couldn't dance, I couldn't play football, I couldn't swim – and it was all because of my heart. I hated it.

'Here, Cam! What're you doing?' Marlon called out from the pool.

Only then did I remember where I was. 'Er . . . nothing. Look, Marlon, I'm going straight home. OK?'

'Are you all right?' Marlon was immediately concerned.

'I'm fine. I'll see you in the park tomorrow,' I called back.

'Oh, OK.' Marlon still didn't sound completely convinced. 'We'll have a good game of football for you to watch tomorrow. We've challenged Manor Park.'

My smile faded. 'I'll be there,' I called out. Without waiting for Marlon to respond, I walked into the changing rooms.

Marlon had automatically assumed that I would be a

spectator. But then what else could I do? I wasn't much use for anything except watching. Everyone, from Travis Cross — our school year's worst bully — to my best friend, Marlon, said so. Oh, Marlon never said so in so many words. He didn't have to. His correct assumption that all I'd do at the football game tomorrow was watch, was enough. That was all I ever did — watch and listen. I was always a spectator, never a participant. I didn't call that living. I was alive — but that was all.

'There's got to be more to it than this,' I muttered from beneath my shower. Warm, foul-tasting water ran into my mouth. I spat it out and closed my eyes. There was a song I'd heard once, a song that I remembered more and more often these days. Not all of the song. Just one line: *'Is that all there is?'*

I clenched my fists until my ragged nails bit deeply into my palms.

I was alive. I was. *Alive!*

I wasn't going to let my heart beat me. I had to do something — anything — to show that my body, my energy, my very existence wasn't just down to my heart. I had to have more control than that. But what could I do? Something for myself. Something that was mine and mine alone. Something that no one else could take away from me. There had to be some way that I could be in control without others telling me what I could or could not do.

I left the shower and went back to my cubicle to get

dressed. What now? I didn't want to go home yet – that was for sure. Home to yet another argument between Mum and Dad. I couldn't stand it. It was as if each of them blamed the other for the way I was. It was driving me crazy. So I'd think of somewhere else to go first. The question was – where?

I walked up my quiet road, dragging my heels. So much for all my big talk! As usual, I'd done nothing. Instead I'd hopped on a bus and headed straight home. I didn't even bother to daydream the way I usually did on my way home. No wild adventures, no safaris, no starship expeditions occupied my mind and my time.

Today I thought about the viral infection I'd caught almost two years ago now. A viral infection that had affected my heart. And now, oh so slowly but surely, my heart was weakening. I'd had drugs and pills and potions up to yahzoo. I had to hand it to the doctors at the hospital – they had tried. But their best wasn't good enough. So here I was, just me and my heart, where every beat was like the tick, tick, ticking of a clock counting down my life.

TICK tick tick ticktickticktick . . .

Chapter Three

News

As I turned the key in the front door, I could hear at once that Mum and Dad were at it again. 'Now there's a surprise!' I mouthed silently, adding, 'I wonder what they're arguing about today.'

As if I didn't know!

Shutting the door quietly behind me, I tiptoed through the hall to the living-room door.

'No, I won't allow it!' Mum raged.

I recognized that tone of voice. It burnt like a laser. I winced, aware of how my dad would react to it. I wasn't wrong.

'Don't talk to me like that. I have some say in this too. And I've weighed up all the consequences. I've listed all the pros and cons. We don't have any other choice—'

'We? This has nothing to do with us. You went ahead and did this all on your own – as usual.' Mum's voice was lemon-bitter.

'You make it sound as if all I was doing was thinking of myself.'

'Weren't you?'

'Of course not.'

'Now why don't I believe that? My mum has a saying – "Never stick your head where your backside can't follow."' Mum wasn't letting Dad get away with anything. 'But that's exactly what you're doing. You're getting us into something we'll never get out of – and you didn't even *ask* first.'

'It's for Cameron's own good. It's for the good of this whole family,' said Dad.

'Because you say so?' Mum scoffed. 'From where I'm standing it looks as if what you want to do is deform your own son . . .'

I nodded grimly. I'd guessed what Mum and Dad would be arguing about and I was right again. I hated always being right. Mind you, I hadn't heard this particular argument before. This one seemed to be a new track on an old CD.

'What d'you mean "deform"?' Now it was Dad's turn to hit the roof and pass right through it. 'How dare you say that? You wouldn't say that if this was a human heart—'

'But that's the whole point. It's not, is it? You want to make our son a pig-heart boy.'

A pig-heart boy? What on earth was Mum talking about? I frowned as I leaned in closer.

'Better a pig's heart that works than a human heart that doesn't,' Dad argued. 'Better that than no heart at all.'

'You think so?' said Mum.

'Yes. Don't you want our son to live?'

A slap, like the crack of a whip, made me flinch as if Mum had slapped me instead of Dad.

Silence echoed throughout the house.

'I'll never forgive you for saying that to me. Never.' Although Mum's voice held quiet fury, there was more than a little hurt in it as well. 'I love Cameron desperately. I'd do anything for him – anything. If I could give him my heart, I would. But I won't let you use him like this.'

'Cathy, don't you think I've thought about this?' said Dad. 'Don't you think I've lain awake at nights thinking about this? I've thought of nothing else but Cameron for the last two years. Our son has a year to live – at most. There aren't enough human organ donors to go around. So we have a simple choice. We can allow our son to have a pig's heart or we can watch our son die.'

'You'd really let them implant a pig's heart into our little boy—?'

'I don't want to see him die,' Dad interrupted. 'And I've been reading up about it. The doctors have been using pigs' valves in heart surgery for years.'

'A valve is different to a whole heart,' Mum argued.

'Not so different. They use pigskin for skin grafts on humans, pig insulin is supplied to diabetics, pigs'-heart valves are used all the time, so why not use a whole pig's heart?'

'It's not the same . . .' Mum insisted.

'What's different?'

'Well, if you don't know then I can't tell you.'

'Look. This is Cameron we're talking about here. Our son. Our only child,' said Dad.

I leaned against the wall and looked down, way down past my feet, past the carpet, to a place far, far below me where I was totally alone. My stomach was churning like a liquidizer. Beads of sweat prickled on my forehead like hot needles.

A pig's heart. What was the phrase Mum had used? Pig-heart boy . . .

'Cathy, it's not as if they go to the nearest pig farm and pick out any old pig. They have pigs which've been especially bred for this.'

'And that makes it all right, does it?' asked Mum bitterly.

'Yes, it does. That's the whole point,' Dad replied.

'Stop it! Stop it, both of you!' I shouted.

I couldn't bear to listen to any more. I turned and raced up the stairs, stomping down with my feet as hard as I could as I ran. I only got halfway up the stairs before I started hurting, so I slowed down, but I didn't stop.

'Cam? Cam, wait,' Mum called out.

I didn't answer. I couldn't. But I wanted to let both of them know that I was here. They were talking about me as if I didn't have a mind of my own, as if I couldn't make my own decisions. How could they? *How dare they?* It was my body. My heart.

I threw myself face down on my bed. I'd barely caught my breath when there came a knock at the door.

'Cam, can I come in?' asked Dad.

'I suppose so,' I muttered.

Dad walked into the room, followed by Mum.

Without preamble, Mum asked, 'Did you hear what we were talking about?'

'I think the whole street heard,' I replied as I sat up.

Dad sighed. 'I'd rather you hadn't heard the idea that way . . .'

'What way?' I asked.

'With your mum and me arguing about it,' he replied.

I didn't see what difference it made. At least by eavesdropping I'd heard the truth as both Mum and Dad saw it. But now they'd change their way of talking. Now they'd talk to me in a way they thought I could understand. A way suitable for a teenage boy – all false smiles and falser promises.

'Cam,' Dad began as he sat down on the edge of my bed. 'Cam, a few months ago I wrote to a man, a doctor, called Dr Richard Bryce.'

I looked across at Mum, who was leaning against the door. 'Who's he?'

'He was a surgeon, but now he's an immunologist specializing in transgenics.'

'Huh? What's that? What's trans . . . transgenics?'

25

'Transplanting the organs of one species of animal into another.'

'Why would anyone do that?'

'Because there aren't enough human organ donors,' Dad explained carefully. 'So people like him are trying to find other ways of keeping people like you alive.'

People like me . . . I winced at Dad's phrase.

'I mean, people who need hearts or kidneys or livers to have a decent quality of life,' Dad added.

I said slowly, 'So you want me to have a pig's heart?'

'I want you to have a heart that will allow you to do all the things you want to do. All the things a boy of your age should do. And that's where Dr Bryce comes in. Transplants are his area of expertise. I wrote to him via a newspaper to tell him about you and your case. I thought he might be able to do something to help you. I also sent him a letter of permission so that he could get your notes from our doctor and the hospital.'

'Why didn't you tell me before?'

'I didn't know if Dr Bryce would want to help you. I didn't want to raise your hopes only to see them dashed again. We've been down this road twice before when we thought you'd be able to get a heart transplant from a human donor – remember?'

Yes, I did remember. How could I forget? Once, I'd even got as far as the hospital, only to be turned back. A greater emergency had required the heart. I had been pipped at the post. Mum and Dad were furious. They stood and ranted at the hospital staff for a good thirty minutes. It wasn't their fault. The heart had been diverted to another hospital. There was nothing they could do about it. And then Mum had burst into tears. No, I wasn't about to forget that little episode – not if I lived to be ninety.

I sighed. 'Dad, I still wish you'd told me.'

'Don't worry about it, Cam. He didn't tell me either,' Mum piped up from the door.

I looked at her. She was so unhappy, so tired and unhappy. This was what I was doing to her. Doing to my family. Tearing them apart.

'So what's happened? Has Dr Bryce agreed to do the heart transplant then?' I asked.

'It's not that simple.' Dad shook his head. 'Dr Bryce has agreed to come and see us to talk about it. I certainly wouldn't agree to it without talking to you first.'

'So when does Dr Bryce want to see me?'

Dad looked from me to Mum and back again. 'He's coming to see you tonight.'

Chapter Four

Dr Bryce

'Tonight? *Tonight!* And you didn't think to tell us before now?' Mum's body was rigid with rage.

'I didn't know myself until about two hours ago. Dr Bryce phoned me at work and asked if he could come and see us this evening. What was I supposed to do? Say no?'

'You were supposed to talk to me and Cameron first.' Mum's voice was getting quieter and quieter. She stared at Dad at that moment almost as if she hated him. I turned away. I couldn't bear to watch.

'I've just told you. I couldn't say anything until I knew Dr Bryce would take Cameron's case and I didn't know until a couple of hours ago. If I'd said something beforehand you just would've got upset for no reason.'

'So you knew I'd get upset . . .' Mum's eyes narrowed. Her voice chilled like liquid nitrogen.

'I thought you might, until you'd had a chance to calm down and really think about it—'

'Don't patronize me, Mike,' Mum snapped.

'Look, Dr Bryce will be here soon. And if we don't present a united front then we can all forget it,' Dad snapped back. 'He's hardly going to take this any further if you sit there glaring at him and making it obvious that you're against the whole idea.'

'Then I'll sit there with a blank expression on my face and I won't say a word. Happy now?'

'If you two are going to argue, can I go downstairs?' I sighed. 'I came up here to get away from you.'

Mum frowned. 'Cameron, that's enough. Don't be so cheeky.'

'I'm not being cheeky,' I replied, bitterness spilling out in my voice. 'I'm just tired. Tired of you two fighting about me all the time. Tired of dreading coming home to listen to yet another quarrel. Tired of being piggy-in-the-middle . . .'

My voice trailed off as I realized what I'd just said. *Piggy-in-the-middle* . . .

I couldn't help it. I started to laugh. Dad's lips twitched. Mum looked wry as she too started to smile. She couldn't laugh, though. But me and Dad were laughing, loud, raucous laughter — unexpected and all the more welcome because of it. Then I burst into tears. It was hard to say who was more shocked — Mum, Dad or me. Mortified, I tried to stop. I tried to choke back the tears but that just made it worse. I gulped hard and tried to take a deep breath, but the tears kept flowing.

They ran down my cheeks and under my nose and into my mouth, salty and unwelcome. I wiped my face with the back of my hands, wishing the bed would open up and swallow me.

'Cameron darling, what's the matter?' Mum flew across the room in a moment.

'Cameron, don't cry,' Dad said, anguished. 'Look, I didn't mean to upset you. If you don't want to meet this doctor then you don't have to. I wouldn't force you to do anything you didn't want to do.'

'No. No. I . . . I w-want to meet him,' I stammered.

'What's the matter, Cam? Why are you crying?' Mum asked, her arm around my shoulders.

I shook my head but didn't speak. How could I answer? What was I supposed to say when, for the life of me, I had no idea why I was crying?

'Cam . . . ?' Mum got no further. At that moment the doorbell rang.

'Dr Bryce,' Dad said. 'Cameron, are you sure you want to see him? Because if you don't, I'll send him away.'

'It's OK. I'm all right now.' I shrugged away from Mum's arm. 'I'll go and wash my face. I'll see you downstairs.'

Without giving my parents a chance to say another word, I stood up and ran to the bathroom. Once there I locked the door. I needed a few seconds of peace. I still had no idea what had made me blub like that. I

30

couldn't remember the last time I'd cried. Where had that come from?

'You're just feeling sorry for yourself.' I scowled at my reflection in the mirror above the basin. 'Stop it! Stop it now!'

I turned on the cold tap and allowed the water to run colder and colder into the basin. Pulling the plunger to set the plug, I waited until the water was almost to the top. Then I plunged my face into it. Instantly my skin began to tingle. I opened my eyes and reluctantly straightened up. That was better. It was just a shame I couldn't stay longer with my head beneath the water. I emptied the sink, then sat down on the edge of the bath. As I dried my face, my thoughts turned to Dr Bryce. Something told me that if and when I met this man, my life would change – one way or the other – for better or for worse. And all I had to do was go downstairs. Or I could call Dad and tell him that I didn't want to meet Dr Bryce and that would be the end of that. Life would go on as normal.

And I'd be dead before my fourteenth birthday.

Or I could go downstairs into the unknown and take it from there. I took a deep breath and headed downstairs.

I scrutinized Dr Bryce and made no attempt to hide it. But, unlike most grown-ups, Dr Bryce didn't look annoyed or try to give a false smile; instead he met my gaze unwaveringly.

'I'm sorry if we seem a bit . . . preoccupied.' Dad glanced at Mum. 'It's been one hell of a day.'

'Please don't apologize.' Dr Bryce waved Dad's apology aside. 'I should have given you more notice that I was coming, but I have to be very careful, as I'm sure you can understand.'

Dad nodded sagely. Mum gave a closed mouth acknowledgement of Dr Bryce's words.

'Why d'you have to be careful?' I asked bluntly. Mum and Dad might know but I certainly didn't. I was fed up with everyone talking around me and past me and through me. It was as if . . . it was as if I was dead already. And I wasn't.

I wasn't.

'Well, Cameron, we've been trying to solve the problem of the lack of human organs available for donation for some years now.' Dr Bryce spoke directly to me, his tone earnest. 'Some doctors are developing mechanical or robotic hearts. Some are working on ways to prolong the life of an already defective heart. My team and I have tried another approach.'

'Pig hearts,' I supplied.

'Pig hearts.' The doctor nodded. 'But a number of animal rights and animal welfare groups don't agree with what we're doing . . .'

'Why?'

'They feel that we shouldn't be experimenting on animals. They believe it's wrong to sacrifice pigs

32

and all the other animals we use in our research to help humans.'

'But you obviously don't believe that,' I stated.

Dr Bryce shook his head. 'I eat meat and I see nothing wrong with using animals in medical research as long as it's done in a humane way. We're not cruel to our animals.'

'Isn't that a matter of definition?' Mum asked.

'Cathy, I really don't think—'

Mum interrupted Dad's saccharine smile: 'Mike, I'm only asking. Or would you rather I didn't?'

I winced. They were at it again.

Dr Bryce frowned. 'I'm not quite sure what you mean, Mrs Kelsey.'

'You say you're not cruel to your animals. But you breed them specifically for the purpose of killing them and using their insides to help humans. Some would call that cruel.'

'Do you?'

'I didn't say me.' Mum shook her head. 'I said "some".'

'Chickens, pigs, cows and sheep are bred all over the world for the sole purpose of being killed to feed the human race. We're talking about domestic animals here. Is it any worse to breed them to save and extend human life? Should they be bred for food and food alone? I guess it is a matter of definition but, believe me, I can sleep at night and I have no trouble looking in the mirror either,' said Dr Bryce.

'Do the animal rights people write you lots of letters then?' I asked.

'Some do. And I don't mind that. Everyone's entitled to their own opinion and I respect that.' Dr Bryce licked his lips before he continued. 'I don't want to alarm you here but you should know what you could be letting yourselves in for. My house has been fire-bombed – twice. We've had faeces through our letter box more times than I care to remember and the house was also flooded when one group put a hose-pipe through our front door. We've had to move three times and as a consequence everyone involved in my project tends to guard their privacy very fiercely indeed.'

'Is that why you didn't let us know you were coming until the last second?' Mum asked.

Dr Bryce nodded. 'And that's why it's crucial that if we do go through with this, none of you says a word to anyone about the nature of the transplant. I wouldn't want you to go through all the things I and the rest of my team have had to put up with.'

'Why do you still carry on?' I asked. 'Why don't you give up and do something less controversial?'

'He's dedicated.' Dad tried to laugh off my comment.

I frowned at my dad. What was the matter? Was Dad afraid Dr Bryce might quit right there and then?

'I can't quit. It's what I was born to do.' Dr Bryce replied to me directly. 'I'm one of the lucky ones who have found the one thing that makes their life complete. I couldn't do anything else, even if I wanted to. And besides, it's the only thing I'm good at.'

Dr Bryce's tone was intense. His steely-grey eyes focused on me without a single blink. I couldn't help feeling that the doctor was trying to tell me something, but I had no idea what. It was as if there was something else, some deeper, hidden meaning to the doctor's words which was just out of my grasp.

'So how does all this work then?' I said at last.

Dr Bryce leaned forward, eager to explain. 'The major problem with xenotransplantation . . .' At my blank look he explained, 'That's what we call it when you take the organs from one species and transplant them into the body of an animal from another species. Anyway, the major problem with xenotransplantation is the risk of rejection. Our bodies are very good at recognizing anything that isn't a natural part of us – including transplanted organs – and getting rid of it. So we had to think of a way to trick human bodies into believing that transplanted organs from other animals really did belong. Several years ago we introduced fragments of human DNA into some pig embryos and implanted them into a sow. When the sow's litter was born, four of the nine piglets had significant changes in their hearts and other organs, giving them key human characteristics.'

I watched Dr Bryce carefully. He'd obviously

given this speech before. It was word perfect, set in layman's terms, spoken without hesitation. No stumbling, no mumbling, just facts – enthusiastically and confidently told. An informative, precise and very detached speech. I wondered what Dr Bryce felt about me or anyone else who might be a possible candidate for this pig-heart transplant. What was in it for the doctor?

'The results were very encouraging so we continued our experiments with a lot more pigs. We're now on our fourth generation of pigs with organs that are more of a match for humans. What we're trying to do is grow pigs whose organs contain human DNA so that when the organs are used in human transplants, they're not rejected,' the doctor continued.

'Why pigs? Why not chimps or monkeys or dogs or cats or cows or something?' I asked.

'Now, Cam, I'm sure Dr Bryce didn't come here so you could ply him with questions,' Dad admonished.

'I did actually.' Dr Bryce smiled easily. 'Cameron has an absolute right to ask as many questions as he likes. And, to be honest, I'd be a bit wary if he didn't.'

'So why pigs?' I repeated. I knew my tone was terse but I wasn't in the mood to beat about the bush.

'It's a very difficult question to answer. Chimps and other primates would be a much better bet in xeno-transplantation. In fact there's only about a two percent difference in the genetic engineering of humans and chimps. They're closer to humans on the evolutionary scale – but that's also the problem,' Dr Bryce began.

I frowned. 'I don't get it. If chimps and gorillas and orang-utans and that are more like humans than any other creatures, why are you using pigs?' I really hoped the doctor wasn't going to talk any more medical gobbledegook. I was having a hard enough time trying to keep up with him as it was.

'My lab and most research projects involved in the same area rely on funding. We only get funding if we can persuade large organizations or wealthy individuals to part with their money. They won't part with a penny if we use chimps or monkeys or baboons because of the bad publicity we'd all get. They're *too* closely related to humans, that's one reason. Plus some types of primate are actually endangered now – so using them is out of the question. Most people would find it totally un-acceptable. But pigs, on the other hand . . .' The doctor smiled drily. 'Pigs are not an endangered species, their organs are very close to humans' in size and, as they're already bred for food, we thought it would make sense to use them in our line of research.'

'And do they work? I mean, pig hearts transplanted into humans – do they work?'

'We've never done one before. We've transplanted pig hearts into a number of chimps and baboons over the years but no humans.'

'And what happened to the chimps and baboons?' I asked.

'After a while, they all died,' Dr Bryce replied without hesitation. 'But we've improved our techniques and developed a new anti-rejection medication since then. And last year we transplanted the heart of a pig into a chimp. That chimp is still alive.'

'So you want to use my son as a human guinea-pig? Is that it?' Mum's voice cracked like a whip.

And there was that word again. Suddenly everywhere I turned, there was that word.

Pig . . .

'Not at all, Mrs Kelsey,' Dr Bryce insisted. 'I wouldn't be here if I wasn't confident that the procedure stood every chance of success.'

'How can you be so sure?' Mum persisted.

'It's not guaranteed,' Dr Bryce replied. 'I can't say I'm one hundred per cent certain of success—'

'But you can't say that about anything, can you?' Dad interjected. He gave Mum a warning look. Her lips pursed in angry mutiny for a moment, but she didn't say anything more.

'I'm hoping that this transplant procedure will become the norm – as common as an appendectomy or having your wisdom teeth removed, but to begin with we have to move very slowly and carefully. If we rush in now, we could set people against us rather than for us,' said the doctor.

'Dr Bryce, how many people do you have in mind for this first operation?' I asked.

'I've narrowed it down to two likely candidates. I'm considering you and a woman in her twenties.'

'Why're you considering the woman?'

'She's strong. She's an artist who has a husband and son. She has a lot to live for.'

'And why're you considering me?'

'You're young and strong and I feel you would derive enormous benefit from the transplant if we were to go ahead. You have your whole life ahead of you if we succeed.'

'And as I don't have much longer to live anyway, neither you nor I have anything to lose,' I supplied.

'Cam!' Mum and Dad spoke in unison. For once they were in complete accord.

'Cam, don't say that . . .'

'Cam, that's not true . . .'

Mum and Dad fell over themselves to deny my words.

'I wish that for once, just once, someone somewhere would *tell* me the truth,' I protested. 'I know the truth already, don't you understand that? I'd just like to hear it from someone else for a change.'

My words echoed in the stunned silence of the room. First the tears, now the outburst. Where was all this coming from?

'You're right of course, Cameron.' Dr Bryce was the

first to speak. 'The transplant does carry its own risks – every operation does – but it's a question of carefully weighing the advantages and the disadvantages and seeing which side comes out ahead.'

'And in my case?' I asked.

'In your case, you have everything to gain.'

'And the only thing I stand to lose is my life,' I said quietly.

'But I promise you I'll do my very best to make sure that doesn't happen.'

'But as you said earlier, you can't guarantee it.'

'No,' Dr Bryce agreed after a short pause.

'Cam, I really think—'

'No, Dad,' I interrupted. 'It's my body and my heart so I have a right to ask questions and say how I feel.'

'What's got into you today?' Dad asked, bewildered.

'I was wondering that myself,' Mum added.

'I realized something today,' I said. 'I'm running out of time. Every breath I take is a countdown. So I haven't got time to pretend to feel happy when I'm not. I haven't got time to keep quiet when all I want to do is shout at the top of my lungs. I haven't got time for any more *lies*.'

'My God . . .' Mum breathed the words, stunned. 'Cameron, we don't lie to you.'

'We never have,' Dad agreed.

'You don't tell me the whole truth though. You leave things out. It adds up to the same thing.' I knew my mum was hurt and upset and so was Dad, but I was too tired to search for the right words to water down my feelings. Prevarication and skirting around the truth took strength, patience and stamina and I was running out of all of them.

'D'you have any more questions for me, Cameron?'

Any more questions? Just a billion and one, that was all. 'Are you going to operate on this woman or me?' I asked.

'That's what I'm here to assess,' said Dr Bryce.

I looked from Mum and Dad to Dr Bryce. That's the end of that then, I sighed inwardly.

'I need to know how you feel about the possibility of undergoing this transplant operation.'

I started with surprise. Was Dr Bryce really still considering me after all the questions and the snapping and the bad atmosphere so evident in the room? It would appear so.

'It's entirely up to you, Cameron. Your parents may sign the consent forms but it's your decision.' Dr Bryce smiled.

This was it. The moment that I had been anticipating – and dreading. But, as my Nan said, it was time to tinkle or get off the potty!

'While Cameron's thinking about it, what about you two, Mr and Mrs Kelsey? How do you feel about it?'

'I have every confidence in you, Doctor,' Dad gushed.

'I want whatever Cameron wants,' Mum replied quietly. And although Mum's answer was very diplomatic, it was still crystal clear how she felt. 'I'm just . . . I just feel that it's a Pandora's box you're trying to open here. I wonder if you've really thought about the implications of what you want to do.'

At my blank look, Mum explained. 'Pandora was given a box and told not to open it, but curiosity got the better of her and she did. The box contained all the evils of the world like spite and hatred and intolerance.'

'But remember, it also contained hope,' said Dr Bryce. 'And that's what I think our research team will give the world with our new methods – hope.'

'How many genetically engineered pigs have you got altogether?' I asked.

'We have over a hundred, but only about twenty are suitable for human organ donation.'

'D'you know which pig you'd use for the transplant?'

Dr Bryce nodded. 'We have two pigs who are particularly suitable – their names are Paul and Trudy – but I think we'd use Trudy. She's very special. I think she's our best bet. And once the first transplant is a success, there'd be nothing to stop us doing more. But Cameron, you have to decide whether or not you want to be the first one to undergo this operation.'

First . . . I'd rather be second or third or fourth. That way, any mistakes they made in the first operation could be put right for the next ones. But I didn't have time left to slip further down the queue. It was go first or not at all.

'I think . . . I think, yes. I would like to be considered for the transplant,' I decided.

'I'll just go and make some tea.' Mum left the room abruptly.

I looked at my dad, who looked down at the carpet.

'Dr Bryce, I'd like the transplant very much,' I said. 'It's quite simple really. I want to live.'

Chapter Five

Decision

'Are you nuts? Are you completely round the twist?' Marlon couldn't believe his ears.

I didn't answer. I bit back the smile tugging at the corners of my mouth.

'You're not going to do it, are you?'

'What d'you think?' I replied.

Marlon stared at me. 'I don't know,' he said at last. 'I . . . I'm sorry I reacted like that. It's just that . . . you took me by surprise.'

I shrugged, then added quickly, 'But this is between you and me, right? You're not to tell anyone, not your sister, not Rashid and Andrew, not even your mum and dad. Promise?'

'I promise.' Marlon raised his right hand. 'What're you going to tell everyone – after it's over?'

'I'll tell them I had a heart transplant – which will be true.'

'And what happens when people ask where the heart came from?'

'Why would anyone ask me that? And besides, if they do, I'll just say a suitable donor was found at the last minute. And I was lucky enough to get the heart.'

'But from a pig!'

'No one will know that – unless you tell them.'

'No, I won't,' Marlon denied quickly. 'But isn't it bound to come out?'

'I don't see why. Dr Bryce said that after the transplant he'd wait six months before announcing it to the media, and even then, he wouldn't tell them my name.'

'But suppose they find out? The newspapers and the TV have ways of digging and digging until—'

'Whoa! We're getting a little ahead of ourselves here. Dr Bryce hasn't even chosen me yet. He said he'd get in touch with Mum and Dad at the end of the week to let them know his decision.'

'D'you want it to be you?'

Eyebrows raised, I tilted my head to one side as I regarded my friend.

'I'm sorry. I guess it is a silly question,' Marlon mumbled.

I shook my head. 'Not really. It's just that you and Mum and Dad and all my other friends are perfectly healthy. From where you're standing, you're going to live for ever. But from where I'm standing, I can't see myself here this time next year.'

Marlon turned away, the way he always did whenever the subject of my life span came up. I tried not to mind,

I really did. After all, Marlon certainly wasn't the first to do that and I knew he wouldn't be the last. It was such a common reaction. Mum and Dad argued. My Aunt Louise always had to go to the bathroom and everyone else turned away or changed the subject – or both. Except for Nan. But then she was always talking about death and dying. She said that at her age it was a topic that interested her! In some ways, it made a refreshing change. It was just a shame she lived over 200 miles away in Bolton. And pouring out my troubles to her on the phone rather than face to face wasn't the same. I longed for someone – *anyone* – I could just *talk* to. Someone who would listen while I said all the things that boiled and bubbled deep inside me but which had never been said out loud. All the things that felt like molten lava just waiting to erupt – and then, watch out! But that person didn't exist. It made me feel alone, and very lonely.

'But from a *pig* . . .' Marlon still couldn't get over it. 'Don't you mind? I mean, I know it's a chance for you to . . . to be healthy and all that, but don't you *mind*?'

'Marlon, if it was the heart of a cockroach, I'd still want it,' I told him straight.

'Yes, but a *pig* . . .'

'Marlon, you're not listening to me,' I said patiently. 'I don't mind. The truth is I don't care. If it means I'll live longer . . .'

'But aren't you afraid that the pig's heart will some-how . . . *change* you?'

'Change me – how?'

'I don't know. Maybe it will . . .' Marlon trailed off, anguished.

I couldn't help it. I burst out laughing. 'Turn me into a pig? D'you think I'll start walking on all fours and grow bristles and turn pink?!'

'Cam, it's not funny,' Marlon fumed. 'You don't know what that thing will do to you once it's inside you.'

'I know it won't turn me into a pig – that's for sure. My brain will be the same and my soul, the thing that makes me *me* – that'll be the same.'

'You believe you've got a soul?'

'Of course,' I said, surprised. 'Don't you?'

'I don't know. I don't know much of anything. You confuse me.'

'I don't mean to,' I sighed.

'I know. But you . . .'

'Go on . . .'

'Never mind.' Marlon looked away.

'Marlon, I'll be exactly the same after the operation as before, except I'll be fitter – that's all. Nothing else is going to change.'

'You reckon?'

I stared at Marlon. For one brief instant I thought that maybe he was on a wind-up, but his expression was deadly serious. 'Marlon, look at me,' I ordered. 'Take a good look.'

Marlon looked me straight in the eye.

47

'Physically, I'll change. That's the whole point. I'll be healthier. But inside, I won't. I mean, of course I will. I'll have a new heart. But inside where it counts – I won't change. Don't you believe that?'

'I guess.'

'It's simple really. This is my chance at life and I'm going to grab it.'

Marlon smiled faintly.

'What's the matter?' I asked.

'You like saying that, don't you?'

'Saying what?'

' "It's simple really"! That's your catchphrase.' Marlon's smile broadened.

'Is it?' I hadn't realized.

'Everything to you is always "simple really",' said Marlon. 'You're one of the brainiest in the class, your house is brilliant, your mum and dad think the sun shines from your nostrils and you're always so cheerful. How do you do it?'

'It's my natural wit, charm and sophistication,' I said, my tongue firmly planted in my cheek. 'Marlon, sometimes you come out with some real rubbish. My mum and dad are always too busy arguing with each other to notice the sun shining from anywhere – including my nostrils. Our house is always a tip and as for being one of the brainiest in the class, it's just that I do a lot of reading. I don't have the energy to do much else. I wish I did. And that's what this is all about. D'you understand?'

Marlon looked at me and nodded slowly. I sighed inwardly. Had Marlon got the point now? Maybe on a very basic level, but how could he or Mum or Dad or anyone else not in the same boat understand just what I was going through? How could they know what it was like to drink in every sight, every sound, every taste, every word around you, because it might be the last time you had that experience? No one else could begin to imagine what it was like to go to sleep each night, wondering if you'd see the morning.

'I guess it's lucky you're not a Rasta . . .' Marlon said wryly.

'Or a Muslim.'

'Or a vegetarian.'

Marlon and I both began to chuckle.

'There you are. My luck's getting better already!'

A strange thought entered my head. At least Rastafarians and Muslims and vegetarians believed in something. What did I believe in − except life and living? Life and living . . . Surely that was enough . . .

'Maybe you'll change your mind when the crunch moment arrives,' said Marlon.

'And maybe I won't,' I countered.

'Cam, are you scared?' Marlon whispered.

I considered the question, then nodded. 'I'm scared in case Dr Bryce says no. And I'm scared in case Dr Bryce says yes.'

'You can't win, can you?' Marlon sighed.

'Not so far,' I agreed sombrely, my smile all but gone. 'Not so far.'

The longest three days of my life followed. Each night I sat at home waiting for the phone to ring. Each morning I was the first one at the door when the letters dropped through the letter box. But nothing. I felt as if I was going quietly crazy. If I didn't hear something soon, my heart would give out from all the anticipation! I found myself wondering about the woman who was the other candidate for the heart. What had Dr Bryce said? The woman was an artist? And she had a husband and a son too. Surely the doctor would give the heart to her. The artist woman seemed to have a lot more going for her than I did. How would Dr Bryce make up his mind? And why couldn't he hurry up about it?

Even Mum and Dad weren't arguing as much any more. A stillness had descended on our house as each of us waited for some word from the doctor. More than once I caught Mum watching Dad, her face an unreadable mask. For me, it felt like the calm before a storm.

And then, on Thursday evening, I came home from school and entered the living room to find Dr Bryce there waiting for me. I searched for clues on the faces of my mum and dad but had no luck.

'Hello, Dr Bryce.'

'Hello, Cameron. How are you?'

'OK.' I couldn't think of anything else to say.

'Would you like to sit down?' The doctor indicated a chair as if it was his house, but my mum and dad didn't even notice. I realized that they were as much in the dark over the doctor's decision as I was. I sat down, my legs suddenly shaky.

'I felt I should be here to tell you of my decision in person,' Dr Bryce explained.

It's not me . . . *It's not me* . . . The words spun in my head. I wasn't surprised. I had no right to be surprised. But the sense of intense disappointment I felt was overwhelming.

'. . . so I've decided that you should have the heart transplant. I thought about it long and hard in consultation with my colleagues and . . .'

I stared at the doctor. His words faded to nothing. I could see his lips move but I couldn't for the life of me hear a word he was saying. It was as if, with a snap of the fingers, I'd been dragged to somewhere outside normal time. I saw Dr Bryce turn to my mum and dad and continue to talk. Dad leaned forward, eager and impatient to catch every word. Mum sat back, her arms folded across her chest. I could even see myself, nodding at what appeared to be all the right moments. Dr Bryce turned and asked me something directly. And with that I jumped right back into the present. I stared stupidly at him. I had no idea what the man had just said.

Dr Bryce smiled as if he knew what was going on.

'It's OK, Cameron. I know it's a lot to absorb in one go. Do you still want to go ahead with the transplant?'

I nodded. I couldn't trust myself to speak.

'Good.' Dr Bryce's smile broadened.

'Will you be doing the operation?' Dad asked.

'Yes. My colleagues and I will be carrying out the procedure.'

'Are you qualified?' Mum asked.

Dad squirmed as the doctor answered.

'Yes, of course. I was a doctor, then a heart transplant surgeon before I ventured into transgenics.'

'And where exactly will all this take place?' said Mum.

'We have a clinic and private hospital wing attached to our research facility. I would anticipate carrying out the procedure there.'

'Where is this research facility?'

'In Yorkshire.'

Mum still didn't look satisfied. She opened her mouth to ask another question but Dad got there first.

'When d'you reckon all this would happen?'

'I was thinking sometime in the next two to three weeks,' said Dr Bryce.

I wasn't the only one to be stunned.

'So soon?' Mum squeaked, dismayed.

'I see no reason to delay now that we've all made up our minds.' Dr Bryce shrugged. 'I'd like to take Cameron into our hospital sometime next week, when we will run extensive tests, and after that we can arrange the date to perform the procedure . . .'

Why did he keep calling it a 'procedure'? That word was beginning to get on my nerves. Why couldn't he just call it an operation like any normal person?

Mum frowned. 'What exactly will you be testing for? I mean, is there still a chance you might change your mind?'

'It is extremely unlikely. We've had Cameron's notes from his doctor and from your local hospital, so I'm not anticipating anything, shall we say, untoward.'

'Are the pigs at your research facility too?' I asked.

The doctor nodded.

'Including the one whose heart I'll get? What was her name – Trudy?'

'Yes, to both questions!'

I considered. 'Can I meet her, please? Can I meet Trudy?'

'Why on earth do you want to see the pig?' Dad asked, astounded.

'I just want to see her,' I said.

'There's no reason for it, Cam.' Dr Bryce's voice was gentle but insistent. 'Besides which Trudy and the rest of her family are kept in a controlled environment. It would take all kinds of wrangling to get you in to see her.'

'If I'm going to get her heart, then I'd like to see her first,' I persisted.

When Dad opened his mouth to argue, I shook my

head quickly. 'No, Dad. Don't try and talk me out of it. I want to see her, I really do. I'm not going to back out or turn into a vegan. I just want to see what I'm getting myself into. *Please*.'

Dad scrutinized me, then sighed. 'You're really serious about this, aren't you?'

I nodded. We all turned to Dr Bryce, whose brows were creased in a deep frown.

'Cameron, I would rather you didn't . . .'

'But I'm going to be there next week anyway, so why can't I?' I pointed out. 'I'm not going to change my mind or smuggle the pig across the Yorkshire moors or anything. I promise.'

'I don't think . . .'

'If he wants to see the pig, I don't see what harm it could do,' Mum said firmly. 'In the light of all the things you intend to do to my son, I think granting this little request is the least you can do.'

'I don't think it's a good idea,' Dad argued.

'But Cameron does and, as you keep saying – this isn't about you or me, it's about Cameron.'

Dr Bryce didn't look at all happy. 'This is against my better judgement, but all right then. I'll see what I can do.' Even now he looked as if he was searching for a way to get out of it.

Mum and Dad glared at each other.

'Are you really sure you want to see Trudy?' Dr Bryce asked intently.

I nodded. I was hardly likely to change my mind in the space of five seconds. I didn't know why I wanted to see Trudy. If Trudy had been human . . . But she wasn't and there was no point in speculating. Trudy was a pig. There were no ifs, ands or buts about it. I couldn't work out how I felt about it. That's why I had to see Trudy. Maybe then my mind would clear and I'd know how to *feel* about it. I couldn't think beyond that. I'd go and see the pig and take it from there.

'Very well then.' Dr Bryce stood up. 'I have to go now but I'll be in touch.'

I watched Mum and Dad leave the room as they escorted Dr Bryce to the door. I could hear them whispering out in the hall but I couldn't be bothered to eavesdrop. The whole situation was so bizarre. I wasn't sure whether I was on my head or my heels. And what would all this do to my family? It already felt as if we were all only holding on by our fingertips. This whole business might be the extra tap on the wedge needed to drive my family apart permanently.

I live in a house full of unhappy people, I thought sadly.

And a pig called Trudy was meant to change all that.

Chapter Six

Trudy

I looked out across the car park to the fields beyond. The fields looked like a patchwork quilt, sewn together using swatches of a host of different shades of green. Some fields were so light as to look yellow, whereas others were so dark they looked almost purple. It was beautiful. I shivered as the chill September wind tried to eat its way through my jacket but I didn't really mind. The fields, the sky, the hedges, even the car park – they all spelt life and hope. We'd had to change trains twice to get to Beaconsridge Station. And if ever a place looked like the middle of nowhere, then this was it. I wondered what the people who lived in Beaconsridge did for fun.

'This is ridiculous. How much longer are we going to have to wait?'

I sighed inwardly as I looked at my mum. For the last four days, ever since Dr Bryce had come to see us, Mum hadn't opened her mouth except to snap or complain. I knew that she was upset about the whole situation, but truth to tell, she was getting on my nerves. And from the look on Dad's face, I could see he felt exactly the same as me. He had tried to parry every complaint with a joke or a smile, but now his smile was beginning to wear thin.

'We've only been waiting fifteen minutes,' he soothed.

'Dr Bryce said we'd be met off the train. The train left twenty minutes ago. I'm not going to stand out here in the freezing cold for much longer,' Mum said sharply.

'Shall we stand inside by the ticket office then?' Dad suggested.

'That's not the point. Maybe we should just get on the next train back home,' said Mum.

'Cathy, for goodness' sake . . .'

'Mum, Dad, I think this might be him.' I pointed to the first car I could see that was coming our way.

I didn't want to listen to another argument. Not here. Not now. For heaven's sake! I was nervous enough as it was. The car I pointed to drove by. But the van behind it pulled onto the station forecourt and drove up to us.

Please let this be Dr Bryce. *Please*, I wished silently.

The driver pulled up alongside us and turned off her engine. She leaned across the empty passenger seat and wound down the window. It wasn't Dr Bryce. It was some woman I'd never seen before. She had dancing dark-brown eyes, framed by a serious, studious face. Her black hair was pulled back into a pony-tail and she wore a white overall.

'Cameron Kelsey?'

'Yes.' I nodded eagerly.

'Mr and Mrs Kelsey?'

'Yes,' Dad replied.

'Who else would we be?' Mum muttered.

'Hi, I'm Dr Janice Ehrlich. I'm Dr Bryce's assistant. Sorry I'm late.'

'That's all right,' I said quickly. I didn't want Mum voicing her opinion about the doctor's punctuality.

Dr Ehrlich smiled. 'Hop in the back and we'll get going.'

I walked towards her, followed by Mum and Dad. When I saw inside of the MPV I was amazed. Comfortable wasn't the word. It was sumptuous. Two sets of black leather seats had been placed to face each other with a small, retractable central console in the middle of each one. Each console had been pushed down to display snacks and a couple of bottles of soft drinks. There was a glass panel between the driver's and the front passenger's seats and those in the back. And the glass was tinted, as were the other windows in the back. No one from outside stood a chance of seeing the MPV's passengers. A quick examination of the display panel in the roof of the car above each back seat showed they could be used to set the lighting in the back, talk to the driver, even play music. What a car! I wanted one!

'What's with the tinted windows? Dr Bryce isn't taking any chances, is he?' Mum sniffed.

'All guests who come to our research centre have to travel in one of our company MPVs. It's a safety precaution. I hope you don't mind,' Dr Ehrlich said.

'Yes, I do,' sniffed Mum. 'But I'll get in anyway.'

We all got in the back of the car. Mum and I sat on one side, Dad sat opposite. Whilst we fastened our seat belts, the door slid almost silently shut.

'Is all this cloak and dagger stuff really necessary?' Mum asked no one in particular.

Dad shrugged. 'They obviously think so.'

The MPV began to move. I turned to look out of the windows. We pulled out of the station forecourt then turned right. Due to the tinted glass, the sky, the build-ings, even the odd person we saw along the way had all taken on a dark grey tinge. I reached up to press the button to switch on the light on my side of the car. I thought the light would help make the back of the MPV seem less shadowy and sombre. It didn't. The yellow light cast from overhead was pale and sickly. Mum, Dad and I sat in an uneasy silence as the car travelled on.

'This is ridiculous,' Mum muttered. 'Anyone would think this was *Mission Impossible* or something.'

Dad and I tittered and even Mum smiled, but it

didn't last long. And still the car kept moving. Mum glanced down at her watch. I did the same. Forty minutes had passed. Mum reached up to press the button on the intercom above her head.

'How much longer before we get there?' Mum asked, irritation lending an edge to her voice.

'Not much longer now, Mrs Kelsey,' Dr Ehrlich's cheerful voice rang out. 'Another two kilometres and we're there.'

With a huff of frustrated indignation, Mum took her finger off the intercom button. A few minutes later, the MPV came to a gentle stop. The doors on both sides of the car slid open. The sudden change in light made me blink rapidly. Dr Ehrlich hopped out first. I undid my seat belt and hopped out, feeling the uneven bump of the gravel beneath my feet.

'Thank goodness for that,' said Mum as she descended from the car with Dad's help.

'Here we are. Safe and sound.'

Mum and Dad exchanged a glance. I knew what they were thinking because I was thinking it too. Dr Ehrlich's constant cheery manner was beginning to get a bit wearing. I took a good look around. Green field after green field rolled away from us in every direction. The only relief to the landscape came from the darker green of the hedges that marked the perimeter of some of the fields. The fields reached out to the horizon. The only building in sight was the building directly behind us. I turned to give it a closer look. It was huge, like an old school building. The two security guards who stood outside the entrance to the building eyed our group speculatively.

'This way.' Dr Ehrlich strode towards the entrance, beckoning to us as she went. Mum and Dad led the way, followed by me.

Entering the building was like entering another world. What had looked like an old school building from the outside was like something from a science fiction film on the inside. The reception area was completely enclosed by glass walls. There were a number of solid wooden doors beyond the glass walls, but each door was protected and controlled by an electronic keypad. The reception area was bright and airy with plenty of plants, each of which was at least a metre and a half high. Two burly men in uniforms sat at the reception desk. They were all smiles when they caught sight of Dr Ehrlich.

'Hello, Janice. You made good time,' said one of the men.

'You know me,' Dr Ehrlich replied. 'I don't hang about!' She turned to my parents. 'You'll have to sign in, I'm afraid. You too, Cameron. Or should I call you Cam?'

I shrugged. 'Whatever. I don't mind.'

As we all signed our names in the visitors book, the man who had joked with Dr Ehrlich smiled at my dad and said, 'D'you know the real reason why we black out all the windows of the van? It's so you won't see Janice's terrible driving!'

'Thanks a lot, Chris!' Dr Ehrlich said indignantly. But the smile in her eyes showed that she'd heard it all before and didn't mind his teasing.

She walked over to the reception door which led to the rest of the building and placed the pass hanging from a chain around her neck against a black control pad with a flashing red light. The door clicked open immediately.

'This way. This way.' Dr Ehrlich waved us on through the door. Walking briskly around us, she led the way through another security door, then down a long corridor with closed doors on either side of it.

'Dr Bryce asked me to show you around our lab before you see Trudy and the others. He'll meet us at the pens.' Dr Ehrlich opened a door about halfway down the long corridor.

We entered a large, square room with long benches and tables covered with test-tubes and burners and centrifuges and PCs and a lot more equipment that looked very scientific, but I didn't have the first clue what any of it was used for.

'This is one of our labs which deals with perfusion.'

'What's that?' I asked, hoping fervently that Dr Ehrlich wasn't going to use jargon that would whiz straight over my head! I didn't want to be blinded with science and words I'd never heard before.

'In this context perfusion is the process of passing blood through an organ or tissue – in this case the heart,' she explained.

I looked around with interest. 'What's that?'

Suspended in a tank, attached to a number of tubes, was a beating heart. I walked over to it immediately. I'd seen pictures of healthy hearts beating. Healthy hearts were very red and beat with a strong, regular rhythm. This heart was in trouble. It was almost black and its beat was erratic and irregular.

'That's a normal pig's heart being flushed with human blood. We're trying to simulate a transplant operation using the heart from a non-genetically treated pig.'

'It's not going very well, is it?' I said.

'No, but we know why. As I said, this is an untreated, normal pig's heart. It can't absorb any of the oxygen from the blood it's pumping. This heart will stop beating within an hour at most. What we're doing is analysing the process at every second to compare it to the heart of a genetically altered pig pumping human blood. It's an experiment for comparison.'

'How long will the heart of a genetically altered pig beat for under the same circumstances?' Mum asked.

'So far, the longest time has been eight months.'

'That's not very long,' Mum said quietly.

Dad looked at her and glanced away again.

'Ah yes, but that heart hadn't been treated with our new anti-rejection therapy. We made a breakthrough several years ago. Dr Bryce has discovered a complement blocker which would—'

'A what?' I interrupted.

'Sorry.' Dr Ehrlich smiled. 'It's like this. The major problem with any transplant surgery is the human body rejecting the transplanted organ. There's one particular part of the immune system that's most responsible for attacking transplanted organs. It's a protein known as complement. Complement is produced by the liver and what it does is destroy any alien cells it might find in the body by punching a hole in them. Complement is like a battalion of soldiers who never sleep. They whiz around the body on a search-and-destroy mission.'

'How does this complement stuff know which ones are alien cells and which ones aren't?' I asked.

'That's a very good question. Well, your body prevents itself from being attacked by its own complement by placing molecular markers on the . . .'

At my blank look, Dr Ehrlich shook her head ruefully. 'Sorry, I'm getting ahead of myself again, aren't I? Basically, your body has a way of placing special markers on its own cells to let the complement know that those cells aren't to be touched. It's like telling the complement that the cells are on its side. What Dr Bryce has done is find a way to add these same markers to the

DNA of the pigs we keep. That's why Trudy is our best bet for this operation. Her heart is perfect!'

'But isn't all this a case of fools rushing in where angels fear to tread?' Mum asked.

'I don't understand . . .' Dr Ehrlich frowned.

'All this . . . genetic engineering. I mean, you scientists are sailing full steam ahead into areas you know nothing about.'

'Mum, it's all right. This isn't *Jurassic Park!*' I said, more to lighten the tension that crackled from Mum than for any other reason.

'But that's exactly my point,' said Mum. 'It's a similar idea, isn't it? None of you doctors and scientists know exactly what you're letting the rest of us in for.'

'Mrs Kelsey, I can assure you—'

'But that's just it. You can't. And neither can Dr Bryce. He made it very clear that there are no guarantees. I read somewhere that there have been cases of . . . super mice! Mice that were injected with the DNA of a rat and grew to an abnormally large size.'

I looked at Mum in surprise. Where had she read that?

'But I also read that they tried to breed super pigs and the poor pigs ended up blind, diseased or much too heavy for their own legs to support them. How d'you know that what you're doing now won't have repercussions further down the line? How can you be sure of what you're doing? How d'you know that some defect in these pigs won't appear maybe five or ten or fifty years later on? And what about the possible diseases that pigs may carry? There may be diseases that a pig can take in its stride which would be lethal to us humans. I read that a number of scientists now believe AIDS originated in monkeys and somehow jumped across the species barrier to us humans. And what about BSE? We now know that mad-cow disease can infect humans as Creutzfeldt-Jakob disease. And what about the flu? I read that every few years a new strain of the flu appears because it mutates in pigs and ducks and then we humans suffer the consequences. So how d'you know you won't be importing a retro-virus into my son when you put a pig's heart in his body?'

I stared at Mum. This was the first time I'd heard any of this.

'You're not the only one who looks things up on the Internet,' Mum told me, her tone defensive.

'All I can say is we're doing our best to make sure that we tackle or are at least aware of every potential problem,' said Dr Ehrlich.

'But as you said – you can't guarantee it.'

For the first time since we'd met her, Dr Ehrlich wasn't smiling. 'No, we can't.'

Mum nodded slowly. 'That's what I thought.'

'But Dr Bryce wouldn't be considering a xenograft if he didn't truly believe that it stood every chance of success,' Dr Ehrlich argued.

'What's a xenograft?' I asked.

'Animal organ transplants are known as xenografts,' she explained quickly. Mum had all of her attention and it was as if she resented any second spent not arguing Dr Bryce's case.

'This complement blocker you were talking about,' Dad began. 'Has that been tested? D'you know for sure that it works?'

'We certainly do. We tested it on specially treated rabbits and the results were very encouraging.'

'So this complement blocker is your way of trying to make sure that the human body won't reject the foreign heart,' said Dad.

'Absolutely right.' Dr Ehrlich was all smiles again. 'And let me tell you, it works. This way.'

She left the lab and marched briskly to the very end of the corridor, opening up yet another security door. To my surprise, I saw that it was a changing room with lockers and shower cubicles.

'Cam, if you and your dad could strip off your clothes and have a shower.' Dr Ehrlich pointed to one side of the changing rooms. 'Mrs Kelsey, I'll show you to the women's changing rooms.'

'I beg your pardon?' Dad said indignantly.

'Oh, I'm not accusing you of having offensive body odour or anything like that.' Dr Ehrlich grinned. 'But all of us have to have a shower immediately before and immediately after contact with our pigs.'

'You're joking.' I couldn't believe my ears.

Dr Ehrlich shook her head. 'Trudy and the others are very special pigs and we can't take the risk of them catching something and becoming infected.'

'You seriously expect us to shower just for some pigs?' Mum was scandalized. 'And what d'you mean you can't risk them catching something and becoming infected? We're more likely to catch something from *them* than the other way around.'

'I'm sorry, but it's something we all have to do. No one is allowed to see the pigs without showering and gowning-up first.'

'This is ridiculous.' Dad agreed with Mum and I agreed with both of them.

'I'm sorry, but that's the way it is. I'm sure you understand. We have to keep the pigs' environment as pure as possible. You wouldn't want us to give Cameron an already contaminated or infected heart, would you?' Dr Ehrlich smiled. 'Besides, Trudy and the others love all the fuss we make of them. They think it's a great game.'

I frowned. 'Sounds like Trudy and the others get treated better than I do!'

Mum frowned. 'Cam, d'you really want to go through with this?'

I nodded. 'Yes, I do. We've come this far. We can't turn back now.'

'Good. Good.' Dr Ehrlich's smile broadened. 'Once you've all had your showers, go out through the other door and put on one of the surgical outfits hanging up in bags on the wall. Make sure you put on the mask and gloves as well. Mrs Kelsey, your surgical outfit is already hanging up in the women's changing room.'

'Come on, Mum. Let's just get it over with.' I spoke before my mum could have another rant.

The doctor led Mum out of the door. Mum marched behind her without saying another word. I didn't need to see her expression to know what she thought of the way we were being treated. With a sigh, I had a look around. The shower room looked a bit like the cubicles at the swimming baths.

'OK, Cam. Let's get going,' said Dad.

We each went to our own cubicles. I stripped off and hung my clothes carefully on the two pegs in the cubicle.

All this to see some pigs! It was bizarre. With each step, with each passing moment, I was getting drawn deeper and deeper into this other world. A world of hope and dreams all tied around the strangest set of circumstances – and a pig named Trudy. I left the cubicle and headed for the showers. From the sound of it, Dad had beaten me to it. Adjusting the temperature in my shower cubicle, I still couldn't believe what I was doing. Anyone would think I was going to operate on the pigs, for goodness' sake! All I wanted to do was look at them – at Trudy in particular.

Still, the water felt warm and soothing against my

skin. I closed my eyes, allowing the water to play over my face and body. Each drop beat a tiny tattoo against my skin. For once, I wasn't aware of my heart. The world was the sensation of warm, running water. And it was so peaceful, so good. I smiled, but my smile faded into sadness. For a brief but welcome moment I had forgotten why I was there in the first place.

I stepped out of the shower and looked around for a towel. Hanging up next to each shower cubicle was a towel in a polythene bag. Shaking my head, I tore the bag open and dried my skin. Tying the damp towel around my waist, I headed towards the second door. I stepped out into a room so bright that it made me blink a few times. Fluorescent strips covered the ceiling and the walls were an antiseptic white. Dad had already got dressed. I saw the bag with my name written on it. Opening the bag. I put on the green surgical trousers and top. There was even a cap which covered my entire head, a surgical mask and gloves. By the time I was finished there was no part of me left exposed except my eyes.

'What do we do now?' I asked Dad.

Dad shrugged and pointed to a different door to the one we had used to enter. We walked out to find Dr Ehrlich and Mum waiting for us in a corridor we'd not yet seen. Both of them were gowned up but I could see that my mum still hadn't cooled off.

'Ready?'

I swallowed hard and nodded.

Dr Ehrlich led the way down the corridor and we entered a small, white room, empty apart from a phone on one wall with a large red button next to it. At the opposite side of the room was something that looked like a metal door frame. A faint buzzing noise came from it, the same sort of noise a fluorescent light gives off. I could tell from the smell that the pigs were near by. In a strange way, the smell was reassuring. It smelt normal – as normal as pig manure could smell! But at least they weren't dealing with super pigs or pigs who didn't do what normal pigs did!

Dr Bryce was already there, gowned and waiting. 'Welcome!'

I could see from the twinkle in his eyes and the creases around them that he was smiling and happy to see us.

'This way. We each have to pass through the scanner over there.' He pointed to the metal frame. 'Then Trudy is in a pen just beyond.'

'Just a minute, Dr Bryce,' Mum began. 'Is it safe? I mean, there's no chance of any of us . . . catching anything from these pigs, is there?'

'You're more likely to pass your germs on to the pigs than the other way around,' Dr Bryce said, just a hint of a sharp edge to his voice. 'Let me assure you that the pigs and their pens are cleaned regularly. The pens are properly ventilated, the temperature is regulated and our pigs are very clean.'

'But is it safe?' Mum persisted.

'Of course it's safe. You've had a shower and changed into sterile surgical gowns so there's no danger to either the pigs or yourself.' He led the way towards the scanner.

'Why do we have to be scanned?' Mum protested. 'We've already showered and got dressed in these surgical gowns. D'you think I've got some apple sauce tucked under my hat or something?'

'It's just a precaution. And we each have to do it,' Dr Bryce soothed. 'It's just that we have been fooled before and we can't afford to take any chances. We've had someone try to smuggle a knife into the pens before now.'

'What type of scanner is that?' Mum's tone was sharp.

'It scans for metal objects.'

'Using what? X-rays?'

'That's right. But they're of a low dosage.'

'X-rays . . .' Mum was horrified.

'A very low dosage.' Dr Bryce tried to reassure Mum.

'I'm not going through that thing.' Even though I couldn't see all of Mum's face, I recognized the tone at once.

'Mrs Kelsey, I can assure you—' Dr Bryce began.

'No, I'm not setting foot near that thing.' Mum insisted.

'But . . .'

'You don't understand.' Mum looked at Dad and me

and took a deep breath before turning back to the doctor. 'Dr Bryce, I'm pregnant and I'm not taking another step until you turn that thing off and assure me that there's nothing around here that could harm my baby.'

I stared at Mum. I couldn't believe it.

Mum was going to have a baby.

Why hadn't she said anything before now? How could she and Dad keep it a secret? I was going to have a brother or sister. Pure joy erupted in me like an exploding volcano. *I was going to have a brother or sister.*

'Dad, why didn't you tell me?' I grinned.

But Dad wasn't smiling. He was watching Mum. 'I didn't know, Cam. I'm just as surprised as you are,' he replied quietly.

Dad had a look on his face I'd never seen before. And all at once the look was gone and his face was a mask. His face looked as if it would crumble if he tried to smile or frown or even speak now.

'Congratulations.' Dr Ehrlich beamed at Mum. 'When's the baby due?'

'In the New Year – April,' Mum replied.

I noticed that she still hadn't looked at Dad. And Dad hadn't taken his eyes off her.

'Congratulations, Mrs Kelsey,' Dr Bryce said. 'And let me assure you, you're perfectly safe. I'm sure the scanner would do your baby no harm at all, but as these are exceptional circumstances, I'll have it switched off for you.'

Dr Bryce walked over to the phone, picked it up and immediately started talking into it. Within a few seconds the scanner buzzed loudly, then the buzzing stopped.

Dr Bryce smiled. 'Go ahead, Mrs Kelsey.'

Mum walked through the scanner but I could tell she still wasn't too happy about it. Dr Bryce spoke into the phone again and the scanner was re-activated. 'I've told them that I'll let them know when we're ready to leave the pigs, so they'll turn the scanner off again for you,' he told Mum as he put the phone down.

'We'd best get going,' Mum said.

I walked through the scanner with Dr Bryce. Dad was a step or two behind us.

'Mum, that's great news.' I grinned at Mum.

'Yes, it is.' She smiled back at me.

Beyond the room there was a short corridor which bent round to the right. As we turned the corner, there were medium-sized pens lined against one wall, each one sectioned off from its neighbour by solid partitions of about a metre high.

'This is Greta,' Dr Bryce announced as we passed the first pig. 'She is Trudy's grandmother. When Greta became pregnant, we implanted some of her embryos with human DNA.'

I stared at the pink pig who totally ignored us, her snout in the food trough that lined one side of her small sty. I would have stayed longer to watch her but Dr Bryce swept on.

'And here she is! Our star – Trudy! Trudy is one of the fourth generation of pigs that have key human characteristics to some of their hormones. We truly believe that Trudy is as close as we've come to having a viable heart for transplantation into a human being.'

Well, Cameron – this is it. Keep your own heart and count every beat in case it's your last. Or have a heart transplant. Simple.

I watched as the huge pig came whiffling up us. Trudy looked straight at me. I looked back at her. She was going to die so that I could live. I told myself that pigs died every day to make bacon and pork pies and chops and sausages. This wasn't any different – except for the fact that I'd seen the pig first.

She was going to die so that I could live. Wasn't that a fair exchange?

So why did I feel so . . . guilty? More than guilty, I felt horrible – almost like a murderer. I told myself not to be so stupid. Trudy was just a pig. Just a pig . . . The words sounded like an excuse in my head.

Just a pig . . .

People always used that argument whenever they wanted to use and abuse animals – or even other people. Part of the excuse used to justify slavery was that we black people were 'less than human'. And the Nazis said the same things about Jewish people. Like Mum said, it was such a convenient excuse. If other people and animals were different but *equal*, then you had to treat them with the same respect that you wanted for yourself. Different but 'less than' was an entirely different proposition. To some people, animals were 'less than' human in the way that tables and chairs were 'less than' human.

It all boiled down to what I believed. And the trouble was, I did believe that animals had rights – just the same as we humans. So what was I doing here? I had the answer to that one. I was trying to save my own life. And what did that make me? Someone who was the biggest hypocrite in the world, or just someone who was desperate?

But what about Trudy? What was her choice? If she hadn't been specifically bred to help me and others like me, she would've ended up as someone's Sunday roast or morning breakfast. If only there was some way she could help me without paying for it with her life. Somehow it didn't seem fair. It didn't seem right to assume that we could treat her like this, just because she couldn't protest – at least not in a way that we humans could understand. As I watched the pig, I began to wonder if seeing her wasn't a mistake.

'Hello, Trudy,' I said. 'My name is Cameron.'

It felt so weird. I shook my head, wondering what on earth I was doing. What had I hoped to achieve?

'What's she like, Dr Bryce?' I asked.

'Trudy?'

I nodded.

'Oh, she's a fine pig. She used to boss all her brothers and sisters around until we separated them off. She's independent and strong and extremely intelligent. She can be a bit stubborn . . .'

I smiled. 'You mean, pig-headed!'

Dr Bryce laughed. 'Yes, exactly. Pig-headed – but she's got a heart of gold.'

A heart of gold . . .

'And if you did operate, when would that be?' I asked.

'Just as soon as we could arrange it,' Dr Bryce replied immediately. 'You still want to go ahead?'

The silence stretched on and on as everyone waited for my answer.

I looked at Dad. He'd started the ball rolling but, from the look on his face, I think he was beginning to wonder what he'd let us all in for. I looked at Mum and reached my decision. 'More than ever,' I replied.

It was simple. I had to live now. I had to live long enough to see my brother or sister. Mum was pregnant, maybe even with more than one! It would be terrific if Mum had twins. And with Trudy's help I would be able to see them and help Mum and Dad look after them. I couldn't wait.

I looked at Trudy. If I'd been alone, I would've hugged her and thanked her properly. She looked straight at me. And I hoped she knew what I was thinking. And I prayed she didn't mind. I looked at Dad and

77

turned back to Mum. Now Dad was looking everywhere but at Mum and I could feel the tension between the two of them. And slowly the joyous feeling that swirled within me dissipated, to be replaced by something less pleasant.

My stomach churned and turned like a tumble-drier and I actually felt sick. Seconds passed before I realized what was wrong. For the first time since Dr Bryce had come into our lives, I was afraid. Not of the transplant operation – although that was scary enough – but I was afraid of what would happen afterwards. Once the operation was over, what would happen to my family? I couldn't help feeling that my family was disintegrating before my eyes and there was nothing I could do about it.

Chapter Seven

Talking

On the train, all the way home, no one said a thing that wasn't a monosyllable. I tried to get Mum and Dad engaged in conversation but I was flogging not just a dead horse, but a rotting one. Mum and Dad had a lot to talk about but there was no way they were going to do it in front of me.

At last we were home.

'I'm going to work on my Heinkel 111, if anyone wants me.' Dad didn't bother to wait around to see if anyone did want him. He headed straight into the front room and shut the door behind him.

Mum watched the front-room door quietly close, her expression grim. 'I'm going to watch the news.' She went into the living room.

I watched in dismay as doors closed around me. This couldn't happen – not now. I wasn't sure what to do. Unhappily, I trailed after my mum. Opening the door, I saw her sitting on the sofa, staring at the TV.

'Mum, shall I make dinner tonight?'

'No, I'll make it in a minute. I just want to watch the news first.' Mum continued to stare at the TV.

With a sigh, I turned round to go up to my room. Mum called me back. 'Cameron, wait.'

Mum stood up and slowly walked up to me. Wrapping me in a bear hug, she said, 'I love you. You know that, don't you?'

Waves of embarrassment washed over me. 'Get off, Mum!'

Mum let me go and smiled. 'I love you very much. I just wanted you to know.'

I shuffled. 'I know.'

'I don't want you to think that this new baby is in any way . . . a replacement.'

'I know that too,' I said, surprised. 'It's an addition, not a replacement. Besides, I'm not going anywhere.'

' 'Course you're not,' Mum agreed.

'Just as long as he or she knows that I'm in charge,' I said loftily.

'Er, I think you'll find that *I'm* the one who's in charge, not you.' Mum flicked my chin.

'Mum?'

'Yes.'

'Can I ask you a question?'

Mum smiled. 'Since when have you needed to ask if you could ask?!'

'Mum, I'm serious.'

'Go on then.'

'Why didn't you tell Dad that you were going to have a baby?'

Mum's smile vanished. She sighed deeply and sat down on the sofa again. 'Don't you think that should be between your dad and me?' she asked gently.

I didn't answer. I stood still, watching.

'Cameron, your dad and I, we have a lot to work out. And we've both had a lot on our minds lately. I didn't want to add to his . . . concerns by telling him about the baby just yet.'

'Doesn't he want another child?'

'Of course he does. We've both wanted another child for years, but it didn't happen. I think we'd both given up hope that it ever would. And when I found out I was pregnant . . . well, it was a bit of a shock.'

'Are you sorry?'

Mum stroked her stomach tenderly. 'Not in the slightest. It's just unfortunate timing.'

I smiled. 'Or the best timing in the world, depending on how you look at it.'

'You're in a half-full mood, I see.'

'Huh?'

'Some people would describe a glass half-filled with water as half full. Others would describe it as half empty. The description is meant to describe the person. If you say half full, you're an upbeat optimist.'

'And half empty means you're a sad specimen!'

Mum laughed. 'Something like that.'

I grinned. 'So I'm a half-full kind of guy!'

'You always were and you always will be.' Mum smiled. 'Now I'd better get dinner ready.'

I went to the door as Mum stood up again. 'Mum . . .'

'Yep?'

'I love you too.' I rushed out of the room before my mum could say another word. My face was on fire and I felt very silly. But I wanted to say it. I wanted to say it very much.

I lay in bed staring out into the darkness. It was so dark, I couldn't tell where the ceiling ended and the night began. So much had happened in the space of one day. It was hard to keep it all straight and clear in my mind. I was going to get my operation – but it was all top secret and hush-hush. I was going to get a heart - from a pig. The faintest trace of unease stirred within me. I stared into the darkness, telling myself off. A heart was a heart – as long as it worked. I couldn't get squeamish, not now. I wanted this operation, didn't I? I wanted to run and dance and swim and do all the other things my friends did without having to weigh up the pros and cons first. And I was going to get that chance. I was going to have the operation and *live*. And the icing on the cake was that Mum was pregnant. Next April, I was going to have a brother or sister. I smiled to myself, wondering who the new baby would look like. I looked more like my mum although I had my dad's smile. But my nan said that boys who looked like their mums and girls who looked like their dads were born lucky. Maybe this was some kind of sign. I was about due for some good luck. And I had the feeling that with this operation coming up, I'd need all the good luck I could lay my hands on.

My head buzzed with thought after hopeful thought. I knew I'd never get to sleep with all the things I had on my mind. I threw back my duvet and swung my legs out of bed. A glass of orange juice would help me to sleep. And maybe one of the chicken legs that Mum had put in the fridge. And maybe a slice of gammon with some English mustard to go with it. I could feel my mouth begin to water. I glanced at my alarm clock. It was 1.30 in the morning. Mum and Dad should be fast asleep by now. Feeling for my slippers, I put them on and tiptoed to the door and out of my room. Gingerly, I crept down the stairs. A sudden, unexpected sound from the front room froze me in my tracks. There it was again. Dad couldn't still be in there. The light was off. But . . . but it sounded a bit like Dad. What was going on? Why on earth was Dad sitting in the dark? I tiptoed to the closed front-room door. What should I do? Now I was at the door, I could see just the faintest light seeping out from the room. Dad must have switched on his anglepoise lamp rather than the main light. Very gently, I opened the door.

It was Dad. He sat at his table with his back towards the door.

'Dad?' I whispered.

Dad's head whipped round at the sound of my voice. I stared, profoundly shocked. I saw something I'd never, ever seen in my life. Something I never thought I'd see.

Dad was crying.

'Dad?' I didn't know what else to say.

Embarrassed, Dad quickly wiped his eyes.

'Dad, are you OK?'

'I'm fine.'

I inwardly grimaced. A stupid question followed by a blatant lie.

'Go on, Cameron. Off you go to bed,' Dad said firmly.

I wanted to stay. I desperately wanted to stay. I wanted to sit down and talk to Dad and say . . . things. But instead I nodded and backed out of the room, closing the door carefully behind me. I headed up the stairs. I paused halfway up to look at the front-room door. Then I looked up the stairs to the darkened landing. Up or down? In or out? What should I do? With a sigh, I went back up to my bedroom. My hunger for chicken and gammon had vanished. I crept into my bed and put the pillow over my head. If only the rest of the world was as easy to blot out.

Chapter Eight

The Announcement

'Cam, can I borrow your French homework? I didn't get the chance to finish mine,' said Andrew.

I turned to look at him. 'If you ever came up to me and said, "Cam, I don't need to copy your homework 'cos I've done it!" I think I'd faint with shock.'

'Oh, go on!' Andrew pleaded.

'Here you are.' I couldn't keep the long-suffering sigh out of my voice. 'But I want it back before the end of the first lesson. Understand?'

Andrew grinned at me. 'Great. Thanks!'

'Andrew, lend me Cam's homework when you've finished,' said Bran.

'You lot could try doing your own homework instead of copying mine all the time,' I said, exasperated.

'Why have a dog and bark yourself?' Bran said.

My mouth fell open. 'You . . . you certainly can't have it after that!'

Bran laughed. 'Only teasing.'

'Yeah, right,' I sniffed.

The first buzzer had sounded so we had five minutes to get to class. I looked up at the blue sky, dotted here and there with snow-white clouds. It was such a beautiful day. The morning sunshine felt warm and very welcome on my face. This was the kind of day where your slightest wish could come true. All you had to do was ask. It was just a shame we'd be cooped up in a stuffy old classroom until break time. Marlon, Andrew, Bran and I walked across the school grounds to get to class. I looked around at all the other kids and grown-ups milling around. Not that I'd ever admit it to anyone, but I liked school.

Julie and Nina from our class walked right in front of us, their arms linked. They were obviously posing! Why do girls always walk together with their arms linked? It's as if they're afraid they'll keel over if they have to stand up by themselves!

Julie smiled at me. 'Hi, Cameron.'

I could feel my face begin to burn. 'Hi, Julie,' I muttered.

'Guess what? I'm going to be in an ad on telly.'

'Are you? Really?' I said eagerly. 'What ad? When's it coming out?'

'Next week.'

'I'll definitely watch it. I'm not surprised though. You're pretty enough to be on the telly.' Stunned, I stared at Julie. I couldn't believe what I'd just blurted out. Where on earth had that come from? Now all I wanted was for a hole to open up and swallow me all the way down to New Zealand!

Nina started laughing. Everyone was laughing – except Marlon. He just shook his head. He knew what I was like! Sometimes I suffered badly from foot-in-mouth disease!

Julie was smiling at me again. 'Cam, I'm only pulling your leg. I just wanted to see what your reaction would be. And it was worth it!'

Shame! SHAME! SHAME! The word was emblazoned across the sky in huge letters and great god-like hands were coming down from it and pointing directly at me. How could I be such a . . . such a ginormous nit!

Everyone was laughing harder than ever now.

'Oh, right,' I mumbled. Why was I so gullible? Every time someone came up with a cock-and-bull story, I would swallow it hook, line and sinker.

'Cam, I only pull the legs of boys I like,' Julie told me softly.

'Pass the sick bag,' Marlon scoffed.

'You're just jealous,' Julie told him immediately.

Me? I didn't know what to think. I even managed to smile at Julie – but only just. After all, she *liked* me. That made her teasing worth it – almost.

'Cam, can I borrow your maths homework – just to check and see if I've done it right?' Julie asked with a smile.

'Sure.' I dug into my bag. It fell on the floor. I took a

step forward to get it and ended up standing on it. I tried to pick it up but suddenly my hands were all sweaty and I dropped it again. When I finally managed to pick up my bag, you could've fried two eggs on my face and they would've cooked in five seconds flat. I got out my maths homework and handed it straight to her.

'Can I borrow it after Julie?' Marlon asked. 'I didn't get the chance to finish mine.'

'How come you don't whinge when Julie asks if she can borrow your homework?' Bran smiled knowingly.

Andrew stared at me. 'What maths homework?'

Marlon grinned. 'Bran, if you wore a skirt and batted your eyes at Cam, I'm sure he'd lend you his homework without a single complaint too.'

'Bog off, both of you!' I replied, my face hotter than molten lava.

'What maths homework?' Andrew was beginning to panic now.

'Andrew, you can borrow it after Julie,' I told him, exasperated.

Julie winked. 'Thanks, Cam. You're a real pal.'

I would've lent her my homework without all the lovey-dovey, goo-goo eyes stuff. I really liked Julie, but at that moment all I wanted her to do was disappear.

She must've read my mind, because she and Nina sauntered off.

'You fancy Julie, don't you?' Marlon teased so that only I could hear him.

'That's a lie. Who said I did?' I scowled at him.

'No one – but my eyeballs work just fine. She obviously likes you as well. Why don't you ask her out?'

I looked around quickly, but Andrew and Bran were too busy talking to hear our conversation. They were discussing how best to copy my homework.

'So why don't you ask her out?' Marlon repeated.

'Shush! Keep your voice down,' I begged. 'Besides, if she said yes, I'd think it was because I'm ill. And if she said no, I'd think it was because I'm ill.'

Marlon gave me a look. 'It must be hard work being you!'

'It is,' I agreed. 'Oh, before I forget, here you are.'

I dug into my bag and took out a crumpled piece of paper.

'What's this?' asked Marlon.

'The maths homework. I copied it out for you.'

Marlon grinned at me and snatched it out of my hand.

'You're welcome,' I said drily.

'Oh, Cameron, can I have a word?' I turned my head. Sticky Stewart, our class teacher, came running up to me.

We all called him Sticky behind his back because he was tall and lanky and reminded everyone of a stick insect. To be honest, I was the one who'd come up with the nickname. I'd only meant it as a joke; I hadn't expected it to take off the way it had.

'Yes, sir?' I frowned.

'Can I have a word?' Mr Stewart repeated. He looked pointedly at Marlon, Andrew and Bran, who were walking with me. 'In private.'

'Cam, we'll see you in class,' Marlon said to me, giving the teacher a suspicious look.

I watched as my friends walked away, before turning back to the teacher.

'I've heard from your mum and dad that you'll be away from next week and for some considerable time.'

I froze. What had Mum and Dad said? And why hadn't they warned me first?

'You're going to have a heart transplant – right?'

I nodded.

'Would you mind if I told the rest of the class? I'm sure they'd all like to join with me in wishing you the very best of luck.'

'What else did Mum and Dad say?' I asked.

Mr Stewart raised his eyebrows. 'That was it really. Why? Is there anything else?'

'No. No,' I said quickly.

'So, can I tell the class?'

I shrugged. 'Yes, I guess so.'

'Good! Good!' Mr Stewart beetled off before I had a chance to change my mind – which I was just about to do.

He bounced across the school grounds with that loping, leaping walk of his and I knew that even if I ran after him, I'd never catch up with him.

What was wrong with letting the class know that I was going to have a heart transplant? Only Marlon knew the true, full facts and he wouldn't say anything. So why was I so upset about the rest of the class knowing about my operation? Maybe I didn't want them feeling sorry for me. Maybe I didn't want them thinking I was even more feeble than I really was – but that was silly. You could be superduper fit and still need an operation. Look at all the footballers and boxers and the like who had operations all the time. So why was I so upset? Still trying to work it out, I made my way to class.

I was in the corridor, only about three metres away from my classroom, when I saw the worst face in the world. I didn't bother to hide the groan that passed through my entire body.

'Look who it isn't! Mr Muscles himself!'

'Here we go again,' I sighed.

Travis Cross, the year hard–nut, had spotted me and was now heading straight for me, followed by his cronies. Just behind him, Marlon came out of the classroom.

'What d'you want, Travis?' I asked wearily.

'A look at a real, live, walking, talking weed,' Travis told me.

'Travis, haven't you got something better to do?' Marlon scoffed. 'Like stick your head in a food processor or something?'

'Marlon to the rescue again.' Travis gave me such a look of contempt that I flinched in spite of myself.

'I can take care of myself,' I told him – and Marlon.

'Yeah, right!' Travis and his morons creased up laughing at that. 'One puff and we could blow you over. Blow you over? Blow you down the corridor more like!'

'You can try,' I said, squaring up to him.

'You're not even a challenge,' Travis said with disgust. 'It'd be like taking sweets from a baby – hardly worth my while.'

'Bog off then!' Marlon told him.

Travis carried on walking, deliberately barging into me. And to my shame he did almost knock me over. Marlon rushed forward to help me. I brushed him aside as I straightened up. 'I'm all right,' I said impatiently. 'Don't fuss. I'm OK.'

Marlon backed off immediately. 'Come on then, before we're late,' he said.

I turned to watch Travis and his friends laughing as they sauntered down the corridor. At that moment, I really hated Travis and his friends. I followed Marlon into the class, wondering if I'd always be so ineffectual. Travis was right. I was a weed.

'How're you feeling?' Marlon asked.

'Fine,' I said brusquely.

Even though I was reading through the last remaining piece of homework I'd been left with, I could sense that Marlon was still watching me. I frowned at him. 'What's the problem?'

'Cameron, whatever happens . . . we will always be friends, won't we?' said Marlon.

'Where did that come from?' I asked, surprised.

'We will always be friends, right?'

'Of course,' I replied. 'Why would we stop being friends?'

And at that moment Mr Stewart entered the room. 'Settle down, everyone,' he called out.

'You're my best friend, Cam,' said Marlon. 'I wouldn't want anything to change that.'

'Marlon, why—?'

'Quiet, please. I SAID, QUIET PLASE!' Mr Stewart yelled at the top of his lungs to make himself heard.

'I just wanted to say—' Marlon whispered to me.

'I'm sorry, Marlon. Am I disturbing your conversation?' Mr Stewart was a sarky old trout – but at that moment he did make me laugh.

'Sorry, sir,' Marlon mumbled.

'That's better.' Mr Stewart nodded with satisfaction. 'Now then, I have an important announcement to make. This is Cameron's last day at school for a while. He's going into hospital next week to have a heart transplant.'

Marlon gasped beside me. I glanced at him, then found it hard to turn away from the shocked expression on his face.

'So I'm sure you'll all join with me in wishing him a speedy recovery and I know we'll all keep him in our thoughts and our prayers.'

I bent my head, wishing the teacher would shut up. He was embarrassing me something chronic. I scowled down into my lap as he wittered on.

'And maybe some of us could come and visit you while you're in hospital,' he suggested. 'Would you like that, Cam?' I looked up and smiled wanly. I couldn't think of anything I'd hate more. It was bad enough that the teachers and my friends already treated me as if I was about to snuff it at any moment, without them seeing me in hospital after a major operation. No, thank you very much.

'Cameron, would you like to come to the front of the class and say a few words?'

A few words? How about two words? Bog off! No way! Go away!

'No, thanks,' I said aloud.

How could he? How could he show me up like that? Say a few words in front of the whole class? Was he nuts?

Mr Stewart smiled. 'Are you sure?'

And the more he smiled, the more I scowled until I felt as if the anger inside me was about to make me pop like a balloon.

'Are you really sure?' Mr Stewart fixed me with what he obviously thought was his most encouraging smile.

I stood up. OK, he'd asked for this and was going to get it!

'Cameron! What're you doing? Are you feeling all right?' Marlon whispered urgently. He pulled on my sleeve but I shrugged him off. Mr Stewart wanted me to talk to the rest of the class and that was exactly what I was going to do. I walked to the front. Mr Stewart was positively beaming at me now. I turned my back on him to face the class.

'I'm due to have a heart transplant operation next week . . .'

Mr Stewart scraped his chair across the floor to sit facing me with the rest of the class. 'Sorry!' he said in a stage whisper. 'Carry on, Cameron.'

'I've been doing some reading about exactly what happens when you have a heart transplant,' I continued. 'First they take a razor-sharp scalpel which is like a knife with an ultra-thin blade. And then they slice into your skin from just below your collar bone all the way down to here.' I stuck my finger in my belly button. I didn't think they'd cut down that far but I wasn't going to stop now. 'And then they take a sharp saw, like a hacksaw, and they saw your breast bone in half. And then they use a thing like a clamp to pull your breast bone apart so they can get at your heart . . .'

'Cameron, this isn't exactly what I had in mind.' Mr Stewart leapt to his feet, appalled.

'I'm sorry, sir. I thought you wanted me to tell everyone about heart transplants. I'm getting to the good bit now.'

'No, Cameron. I think that's quite enough,' Mr Stewart said firmly.

'But I don't understand, sir . . .' I feigned ignorance. 'What *did* you want me to talk about?'

'I thought you could talk to us about . . . about what will happen next week, without being quite so graphic,' he said.

I looked around the classroom. Mr Stewart wasn't the only one who was looking appalled. I'd only meant it as a joke, but more than one shocked face stared back at me. Julie's eyes glistened and her lips were turned down. Andrew actually looked sick. Even Marlon looked upset. My joke had backfired. I took a deep breath.

'Look, it's not as bad as it sounds,' I started again. 'It's just that our hearts are very well protected. When you think about it, we can do without most of our bodies if we have to − except our brains and our hearts. Our brains are well protected in our skulls and our hearts are protected behind our rib cage. So they have to move the rib cage out of the way to get to the heart, that's all.' Mr Stewart sat down again slowly. I carried on. 'And think about it − every other part of our body gets to rest. Even our brains rest to a certain extent when we're asleep. But not our hearts. Our hearts have to keep pumping, pumping, pumping. The heart is a very strong muscle that lasts us all our lives. But sometimes, like in my case, something goes wrong with it and it has to be replaced. So that's what's going to happen to me next week.

When they replace my heart, I'll be unconscious and that's the way I'll stay until the doctors have finished, so I won't feel a thing. And besides, heart transplants are common operations now. They're as common as . . . as taking out your appendix.'

I knew that wasn't quite true but never mind. It had the desired effect. Mr Stewart was beginning to smile again and everyone else looked a little less worried. It was strange, but in that moment it was as if everyone in the class was on my side. It was as if everyone was worried about me and rooting for me. It was a good feeling. I was cared about. I belonged.

'I'm sorry about before. I didn't mean to scare anyone,' I mumbled.

'That's all right.' Mr Stewart's lighthouse beam was back. He leapt up and faced the rest of the class. 'Let's give Cameron a big round of applause.'

A couple of people started clapping, then everyone else joined in. I've never been so humiliated in my life. I scowled at the back of Mr Stewart's head. He had made me very, very sorry I hadn't continued with my original description of a heart operation. It seemed to me that that was all grown-ups ever did. They either talked down to you, ignored you or showed you up something chronic. I just hoped and prayed that I would grow older but not grow up. To be a grown-up was the lowest of the low!

Chapter Nine

Messages

I feel a bit silly. I'm not used to talking like this. Dad hates talking to answering machines. I've never really understood why until now. I don't mind talking to answering machines, it's never bothered me, but this is different. I'm sorry. I'm rambling. I have so much to say, but it all seems so little. Trivial really. I mean, I'm just an average boy with not much going for me. I get good marks at school but, apart from that, I'm average looking – no, I take that back, I'm super-cool looking – of just above average height, I eat average food – but don't tell Mum I said that. I'm pretty much average all over. I'm sorry. I'm rambling again.

Look! Let me start at the beginning.

I'm your brother. My name is Cameron Joshua Kelsey. I know! It sucks, doesn't it? Mum and Nan chose my first name – after my grandad who's dead now – and Dad chose my middle name. The only taste any of them has got is all in their mouth. I mean, Cameron. Yuck! Mum said I can choose your name. The trouble is I don't know if you're a boy or a girl. Mum, says that when she has her scan in a week's time, she's not going to ask what sex you are. So I'm going to have to think about this. I want to call you something when I talk to you . . . Hang on! The camcorder has just nodded on its tripod! I hope that doesn't mean that I'm being boring. Just a sec!

There! That's better. I had to tighten the fixing screw on the tripod. I've focused the camcorder on this chair so I can't move about much or I'll disappear out of the picture.

Disappear out of the picture . . .

That's quite ironic, that. It'd be quite a good joke if it was funny! Let me just sort out my thoughts. It's hard to know where to begin really. It's like this. I'm going to have an operation soon. I've got a bad heart. I caught a viral infection almost two years ago and it's still affecting me. My heart is slowly wasting away. So now I'm going to get it replaced. The thing is, because there aren't enough human heart donors, I'm going to get the heart of a pig. To be honest, the way I feel at the moment, I couldn't care less where it comes from, as long as it works. But no one's had a pig-heart transplant before. Until a few years ago the government had actually banned transplants from animals. I might . . . I might not make it through the operation, and even if the operation is a success, who's to say what will happen after that.

So there you have it. I'm going to have this operation and I don't know if I'm going to be around when you're born or to watch you grow up. So I wanted to leave you something to remember me by. I could've written letters, I suppose, but that's boring and it would take tons of writing. So I decided to leave you a whole load of recordings with my handsome face on them. I thought I'd give you my brotherly advice on life, the universe and everything.

Mum and Dad have promised to stay out of the room while I do this so I can talk about anything I like. And they've promised that if something does happen to me, they won't watch the tapes until you're old enough to maybe give them permission. To be honest, I'd rather you didn't show Mum and Dad these tapes. I'd like these to be just between you and me, but I guess it's your decision.

I had to tell my class about the operation and what's going to happen. I didn't want to. I was forced into it, so I started telling everyone all the in and outs and in betweens. I really upset some of my friends. I didn't mean to do it. It was more to get back at Sticky Stewart — he's my class teacher — than anything else. And I upset Julie. Don't tell anyone but I kinda fancy her. She's gorgeous! I don't want to get all wet rag but I really, really, fancy her. Every time she's around I try to act all sophisticated and knowing but it always goes wrong and I end up looking like a complete moron. I know she thinks I'm a twit, and whenever I try to change her mind about that, I just make things worse.

Just a sec — I just want to check the door to make sure Mum and Dad aren't listening. Here I am — back again! I've got a confession to make — and this is strictly between you and me. If you tell anyone, I'll kill you! I wrote a poem about me and Julie and how I feel about her and how I know that she thinks I'm a class one, grade A-plus nozzle! I'll read it to you. Hang on, it's buried under my mattress.

Now I mean this! I'm only going to read this to you on the strict understanding that you won't tell anyone else. If it got around that I wrote some poetry and, worse still, to a girl, I'd never live it down. Here goes! It's called 'I've Done It Again'. Don't laugh!

Confidence up, confidence down
Act like an angel, look like a clown,
Changing your mind, changing it back.
The quick recipe for a heart attack.

Smile at your blunders, laugh at my own.
This isn't right, I should be at home.
Under the duvet, safe from attack.
Changing your mind, changing it back.

Accident prone, but never you worry,
I'll tell you when you can leave in a hurry.
Making up ground for the sense that I lack.
Changing your mind, changing it back.

I've done it again; proved my reputation.
Is this sorrow . . . or is it elation?
Statements once given I cannot retract,
Changing your mind, changing it back.

The notice I earn is diluted with patience,
The smiles that I give are the scorns I receive.

While I hold my breath and count to one hundred,
You'll tell me a tale I am sure to believe.

Fanciful feelings hiding a fool,
A cog that's not turning, a bottomless pool.
Lend me what's common of which you've a stack.
Then I'll change your mind and I won't change it back.

What d'you think? Dead soppy, huh? That's why I wouldn't read it to anyone else but you. If I can't tell my own brother or sister, who can I tell? I've written some other poems too. One about Mum and Dad's computer and one about Chelsea Football Club — they run things! — but I won't read them out. At least not now. Maybe I will one day. And then again, maybe I'll spare you 'cos they're all as bad as the one I just read out.

What should I talk about now? I'm finding this a bit difficult without really knowing who I'm speaking to. I think I'll sign off here. I'm a bit embarrassed after that naff poem. I'll get back to you.

Chapter Ten

Preparation

'Are you OK, Cameron?'

'Yes, Mum.' I suppressed a sigh. How many times was Mum going to ask me that question?

'Can I help you with anything?' Mum took the neatly folded pyjama shirt out of my hands, shook it out and began to fold it again.

'No, Mum, I can manage.' I pulled the shirt out of her reluctant hands.

'I could . . . er . . .' Mum looked around eagerly, trying to find something to keep her in the room.

'Mum?'

'Yes, dear?'

'I can manage.' I spoke firmly, looking her straight in the eye.

Mum smiled ruefully. 'I'm getting in the way, aren't I?'

'Yes.'

'And I'm getting on your nerves.'

'Correct.'

Mum chuckled. 'I'll leave now.'

'Thank you,' I replied, with sincere gratitude.

'Call me if you need me.'

'I will.'

Mum left my bedroom after one more glance to make absolutely sure that there was nothing to keep her. I shook my head as I added my pyjama shirt to my already full suitcase. That was about the twelfth time Mum had entered my room in the last half hour. And as for Dad – he was out in the garden, weeding something or other that couldn't wait. Grown-ups were so strange.

I took another look at the camcorder sitting self-consciously in the corner of the room. After a moment's indecision I took out the tripod from under my bed and stood it about two metres away. Picking up the camcorder, I placed it on the tripod, looking through the viewfinder to centre the view on my suitcase sitting in the middle of my bed.

I decided not to start the camcorder just yet. I had other things to take care of first. Pushing the new toothbrush down the side of my suitcase, I sat on the lid to close it. It shut quite easily. Sitting on it probably wasn't necessary but it was fun! I looked around my room. This was the last day I'd see it – for a while. I walked over to my window. Dad was on his knees at the back of the garden, digging in his vegetable patch. I sighed as I watched. Dad had been digging in exactly the same spot for the last forty-five minutes. I left my room.

★ ★ ★

'Hi, Dad. What're you doing?'

'Oh hello, Cam. I just thought I'd do a bit of weeding.'

I peered over his shoulder. 'I don't see any weeds.'

'I've got rid of the surface bits, but I have to dig deep to make sure I get all the roots out. There's no point in doing this unless I'm thorough.'

I regarded my dad thoughtfully. What he knew about weeds could be written on a full stop – and we both knew it.

'Will Nan and Aunt Louise be able to visit me in the hospital?' I asked.

'Well, your Aunt Louise is still in Canada, so she won't. And as for your nan - I don't know. I don't think so,' said Dad. 'Can you see your nan letting anyone bundle her into the back of a blacked-out van?'

I had to laugh. I couldn't see that at all.

Dad sighed. 'I just wish we could've told your nan the truth.'

'She knows I'm having a heart transplant, doesn't she?' I asked.

'Yes, but that's all she knows. She doesn't know . . . anything else,' Dad replied. 'Your mum and I are to phone her every day to let her know how you're doing.'

'Can I talk to her on the phone as well? After the operation?'

'I don't see why not,' said Dad.

105

An uneasy silence descended.

'So tomorrow's the big day.' Dad nodded.

'No. Tomorrow I'm just going into hospital. The big day isn't until the weekend.'

'Going into hospital makes tomorrow a big day. It's just that Saturday will be even bigger,' Dad said quickly.

I frowned at him. What was he wittering on about?

'It's not too late, you know. You can still change your mind.'

I turned away from the faint hope I could see in my dad's eyes. 'No. I'm not going to change my mind now.'

'Well, just remember you can. You can even change your mind in the hospital if you want to. Just let me know.'

'D'you want me to change my mind?'

'I didn't say that.'

'But do you?'

'It's your decision – not mine.'

'Dad, what would you do if you were me?'

Dad sighed and stood up. 'I've asked myself that a lot lately. And the truth is, I don't know. I don't suppose anyone can really know unless they're in the same boat.'

'Anything worth having is worth fighting for – isn't that what you've always said?'

'Yes, but sometimes . . . maybe the risk is too great,' Dad said carefully.

'And sometimes maybe any risk is worth it,' I countered.

Dad shrugged. I mentally shook my head. This was such a strange conversation. Why couldn't we both just come out and say what we really thought and felt? Why all this beating about the bush? It was so tiring.

Dad and I watched each other, each of us struggling to find something to say.

'Dad, whatever happens, I'm glad you wrote to Dr Bryce,' I said.

Dad nodded.

'I mean it,' I insisted. 'Thanks.'

Dad nodded again and looked away from me.

'I'll go in and finish my packing now,' I said sadly.

'OK,' Dad said.

Reluctantly, I turned to go back into the house.

'Cameron?'

I spun around immediately. 'Yes?'

'I . . . I . . . never mind. If you need anything, let me know,' said Dad.

'OK.' And I went back inside.

Chapter Eleven

Life Lessons

Well, here I am again. It's been a few days since I last spoke to you and a lot has happened since then. I'm going into hospital tomorrow and I'm going to have my operation a few days after that. It's all very hush-hush. Dr Bryce wouldn't even let Mum and Dad tell Nan what's about to happen. I've already had tests and yet more tests and had more blood taken from my arms than I knew I had. And there are more tests to come. So wish me luck. But that's not all. I've finally thought of a name for you. Mum and Dad said I could choose your name but it was a bit difficult because I didn't know – and still don't know – whether you're going to be a girl or a boy. I don't mind, actually. I guess most boys would like a brother but I really don't mind. Anyway, the name I've chosen for you is – are you ready for this? – Alex. Alexander if you're a boy; Alexandra if you're a girl. But I can call you Alex. What d'you think of that? D'you like the name? I hope so. You're going to be stuck with it for a while! I've passed it by Mum and Dad and they both seem happy with it. Mind you, they're both being so nice to me at the moment, I could've suggested something like Aardvark or Smelly Chops as your name and they would probably have said yes.

So, Alex, here I am! Your brother Cameron. I really do hope and pray that we get the chance to meet and get to know each other. But in the meantime, I'd better get started on my . . . what shall I call them? Life lessons! Yeah, that's a good phrase. Life lessons. Today's life lesson is about parents. I'll be revisiting this topic on a number of occasions, no doubt. That was my newsreader voice! Anyway, back to parents – or, to be more specific, our parents.

Michael and Catherine Kelsey.

What can I say about them? They're not getting on too well at the moment. They are trying for my sake but it's like they're papering over a wall with bumpy and lumpy bits and lots of holes in it. They keep trying to get me to admire the wallpaper, but I can't when I know what's really behind it. You see, the wall spoils the wallpaper but they don't understand that. Does that make sense? I'm not getting too flowery, am I? What I'm trying to say is that they are trying to pretend that everything between them is fine – but my eyes work. I can see for myself that they're lying. And I wish they wouldn't. It makes me feel as if I'm responsible in some way, because I'm ill. My head tells me that Mum and Dad have a lot of things to sort out for themselves that have nothing to do with me, but the gnawing in the pit of my stomach each time they argue makes me want to . . . run away and hide or curl up in a ball on my bed or do something – anything – to get away from them. I don't mean that in a nasty way. I do love Mum and Dad very much –

there, I've said it! I love them very much but they are such hard work.

Dad wrote to Dr Bryce, the man who's going to give me a new heart, and he didn't tell Mum. You can guess how that went down. But then Mum had a bombshell of her own. She was pregnant with you and Dad and I only got to find out because Mum didn't want the X-ray machine to damage you. I can still see Dad's face when Mum said that she was pregnant. He looked so hurt, so unhappy. I wish I'd been a fly on the wall in their bedroom later that night. Since then, they've been very polite to each other but they're not behaving like my mum and dad any more. They are very tippy-toe careful around each other. It's almost as if they're working out exactly what they're going to do and say before they stay in the same room with each other. That's another reason why I'm desperate for this operation to work. If it doesn't, I'm not sure Mum and Dad will still be together when you're born.

I don't want you to blame me for that. God knows I already blame myself enough for the both of us. Anyway, I wanted to talk to you about Mum and Dad, not myself.

The thing to remember about Mum and Dad is that they don't know everything. I'm not saying that they think they know everything. That's not the case. But they do think they have all the answers! But that's not just Mum and Dad really. That's most, if not all grown-ups. They don't like to be told things by anyone under twenty-one. It's as if they believe that the whole world will think they're stupid if we know something that they don't. So watch out for that. It's a real pain.

I'm getting a bit tired now. I think I'll sign off. Wish me luck. This is so strange. I keep talking to you as if you're already here. I like talking to you. You're a great listener! In my mind, I guess I think you are already here. I can't wait to meet you. Let's hope I get the chance.

Chapter Twelve

The Clinic

I sat down on the edge of my single bed and looked around my new room. It was more like a hotel room than a hospital room. There was a television in one corner and a fridge in another. I had my own bathroom and there was even a wardrobe. It was certainly different to all the NHS hospital wards and rooms I'd stayed in before now! So this was what it was like to go into a private hospital! It must be brilliant to have lots of money! I glanced towards the door of my room wondering what was going on outside. Dr Bryce had asked my parents to step outside for a word and they'd been gone at least ten minutes. Part of me couldn't help resenting the fact that the doctor was discussing things about me but not *with* me.

I tilted my head back and closed my eyes. Truth to tell, I didn't want to be alone – not now. Not with only a few days left before my operation. I didn't like feeling this way. I felt like a baby but I couldn't help it. This time next week it would all be over – one way or another. 'Stop it!' I told myself fiercely.

I had to believe that everything would be fine. I had to have faith. If I didn't believe it, then it wouldn't happen. Just at that moment, the door opened.

Mum entered the room, followed by Dr Bryce, Dr Ehrlich and Dad. Mum smiled. 'Hi, dear. Are you OK?'

I nodded eagerly, glad to see them.

'We were just having a discussion about whether or not you should be allowed to keep your camcorder with you,' said Mum.

I frowned. 'Yes. I definitely want it with me.'

'Cameron, that's a little difficult.' Dr Bryce looked concerned. 'For the first few days after the operation you won't be in here. You'll be in intensive care. We have to be very careful that you don't pick up any infections.'

'I want my camcorder . . .' I insisted.

'You'll be too weak to use it.'

'I still want it with me. Maybe one of the nurses could hold it while I talk to Alex.'

'Cameron, I don't want to be difficult—'

'Please, Dr Bryce. That's one of the things I've been most looking forward to – telling Alex how I'm feeling and that I'm still standing. Please.'

Dr Bryce studied me long and hard. 'Very well then. I'll see what I can do.'

I beamed at him. 'Thanks.'

'I haven't promised anything,' he said quickly.

'I know.' I smiled again, knowing I'd won.

'Hhmm!' A trace of a smile flitted across the doctor's

face. 'I'll leave you to settle in. I'll see you in about an hour, Cameron.'

'More tests?'

'More tests,' he confirmed.

During the last week, I'd had more tests at my local hospital than I could count – blood tests, urine tests, allergy tests – they'd even tested my number twos! I'd been hooked up to some strange-looking machine called an ECG or electrocardiogram so they could monitor my heart. I'd had dye pumped into me and so many X-rays taken of my chest, I was surprised I didn't glow in the dark. And now I had more tests coming. Still, as long as the tests meant the operation would work.

'How soon after the operation d'you reckon I can go home?'

'You'll be in intensive care for a while and then we'll keep you in a bit longer than normal to make sure that everything is exactly as it should be. I don't want to state a specific time at this stage. I wouldn't want to give you a timetable and then something happens and we can't keep to it. That would only make you and your parents worry. We'll play it by ear. I think we'll all know when you're well enough to go home.'

And that was his long-winded way of saying he didn't know. I still had 1001 questions, but all at once I didn't want to ask any of them. Not one. I'd ask them after the operation, not before.

I'd wait until my eyes were open and the operation was behind me and I had all the time in the world.

'Hello? Marlon?'

'Cam! What's happening? I came round to your house but no one was there. And then I phoned the hospital, but you weren't there either.' Marlon's tone was close to frantic.

I smiled. 'Marlon, calm down.'

'It's not funny,' Marlon snapped at me. He could obviously hear the smile in the tone of my voice. 'I've been really worried.'

'Sorry.' Marlon really was a worry-wart! What Nan would call a fuss budget!

'Where are you?'

'I'm . . . er . . .' I wasn't sure what to say. 'I'm in hospital.'

'But they told me you *weren't*. I thought . . . you . . .' Marlon's voice was all funny and choked. 'Can I come and see you?'

'Marlon, I'm not in the local hospital.'

'Where are you then?'

'I'm in a private hospital.' I lowered my voice, casting a guilty eye towards the door. 'I'm going to have my heart operation tomorrow.'

Silence.

'Hello?' I wondered if we'd been cut off. 'Marlon?'

'You're having the transplant tomorrow?' Marlon whispered.

'Yes.'

'And you're only telling me now? The day before?'

'Well, I didn't know the exact date myself until recently and Dr Bryce told all of us not to tell a soul, but I know I can trust you.'

'You're having your heart transplant tomorrow?' Marlon repeated, stunned.

'Yeah! Weird, isn't it!'

'Did they find a human donor?'

'Nope.'

'So this is going to be from a . . . pig?' Marlon's voice was getting quieter and quieter.

'That's right.'

Silence.

'Marlon, stop fading out on me,' I said testily.

'Aren't you scared?'

'A little bit . . . anxious.' I shrugged. 'But it's simple. I have to choose between living and dying and I choose to live. Besides, I know it's going to work. This time next week I'll be fine and fighting fit.'

'You're not going to change your mind?'

'Of course not,' I scoffed. 'What kind of question is that?'

'But what if . . . what if it doesn't work . . . ?' Marlon asked unhappily.

'It'll work. And even if it doesn't, at least I will have tried. If I had to do it all over again, I'd do the same thing tomorrow.'

'You would?'

'In a hot New York second.' I smiled. 'So wish me luck.'

'Good luck.'

A strange silence echoed between us. I thought Marlon would find more to say, but I was mistaken. I wanted to say more, but though the words tumbled around in my head, they refused to form proper sentences and come out. Besides, I didn't want to get all mushy and gushy.

'Anyway, I'll talk to you after the operation.'

'Can I come and see you after the operation?'

'I don't think so. I don't think Dr Bryce will allow it, to be honest,' I admitted. 'But I'll tell you what, I'll ask him once I'm out of intensive care.'

'D'you promise? 'Cos I want to see you,' Marlon persisted.

'I promise. I'll phone you after the operation and let you know what happened.'

'Make sure you do. I'll be waiting,' he replied.

'So I'll see you.'

'Yeah. 'Bye.'

' 'Bye, Marlon.' I put the phone down.

I had no idea why I'd done that. I'd wanted to speak to Marlon but I'd ended up saying none of the things I'd wanted to say. But I felt strangely better. Someone outside my family and outside the clinic knew what was happening to me. It made it all seem more real somehow. Dr Bryce, Dr Ehrlich, this whole clinic – I could've dreamt the lot. Somehow, it felt as if I was in the middle of a dream. The whole idea was bizarre enough to be a dream. The only trouble was, I didn't know whether or not I wanted to wake up yet.

Well, Alex, here I am. This is my last message before the operation. I'm at Dr Bryce's clinic now. I had a big breakfast, which is just as well, because Dr Bryce has just told me that I can't have anything else to eat until after the operation. At first I was a bit put out about that, but just between you and me, my appetite has vanished. To be honest, I don't think I could eat anything else. Come eight o'clock tonight I'll probably have changed my mind – but then again, I don't think so. I'm here, setting off on my journey into the unknown. I keep telling myself it's an adventure. Thousands of lucky people around the world have heart transplants and do very nicely, thank you! So why shouldn't I be one of them? And with all the anti-rejection drugs I'll be taking, it doesn't matter that my new heart was in a pig rather than a human first. My body won't know the difference – and that's what counts. I keep telling myself not to worry, I'll be fine.

But I'm scared. There – I've said it.

I'm not just scared, I'm petrified. My stomach feels as if my breakfast is trying to smash its way out.

Come on, Cameron. That's enough. Alex, one day, you and I will watch this bit of my clips and we'll both smile at how silly I was to worry. I can't wait for that. I wish it was tomorrow. No. I wish it was the day after tomorrow. I've never wished my time away before. I want Mum and Dad to hug me, but if I asked them they'd know something was wrong.

How can I tell them that the only thing wrong with me is that I'm so scared I want to cry? They'd think I was a real baby. And then they'd both start worrying about me worrying and we'd all be upset. So, until after the operation, I'll smile at everyone who comes into the room until my jaw aches and if I feel like I'm about to blub, I'll go into the bathroom and lock the door. Grown-ups do that all the time. Maybe I'm more grown-up than I ever thought.

Oh, God, I'm crying now. Wait a minute . . . I need to go to the bathroom.

That's better. This tissue isn't this soggy because I've been blubbing into it. I did blow my nose in it too − honest!

Alex, I hope you don't ever have to go through this. But you won't. I know you won't. You'll be born fighting fit and healthy enough for the both of us. But what am I wittering about? I'll soon be healthy and fit myself. We are going to have such fun. I can't wait.

Chapter Thirteen

Hurt

Someone was calling me – from far, far away. A quiet, muffled voice. 'Cameron . . . CAMERON.'

The voice grew louder and more urgent. It rushed at me like a Eurostar train. 'Cameron. Cameron.'

And then I was awake. It was dark. It took a few moments before I realized that my eyes were closed. But I was awake.

'CAMERON, WAKE UP NOW. CAMERON.'

I was awake.

And my chest hurt. Not badly. But it ached. I tried to take a deep breath, but a spear of pain shot through me from front to back. I instantly held my breath, waiting for the pain to ease – which it did. Slowly, I opened my eyes.

Dr Bryce and Dr Ehrlich were looking down at me. They wore masks and gloves but their eyes were happy. More than happy: their eyes shone with delight. That's when I knew I'd had the operation.

I'd made it. I was still here.

I smiled and the effort exhausted me. I tried to speak but my tongue was stuck to the roof of my mouth and my throat hurt. In fact my throat was hurting quite badly. I hadn't expected that. I tried to swallow but my mouth was as dry as Mars.

'Hello, Cameron.' Dr Bryce beamed at me. Even with the mask over his face I could see that he was beaming.

I raised my hand and put it over my throat.

Dr Bryce nodded. 'Try not to speak. You've had an airway down your throat so your throat will be sore for a day or two.'

My heart's gone!

Only then did I remember. Only then did I dare to think it. My old, rubbishy heart had gone. And in its place – a brand-new, strong . . . pig's heart.

And then it happened. It crept up on me so slowly that I didn't realize what was happening until I was in the middle of it. I was hurting. Well, not so much hurting as aching uncomfortably. My chest ached. My stomach ached. I wanted to cough. I had a headache. My throat ached. I felt sick. There was probably a millimetre-long hair on the back of my hand somewhere that was comfortable but that was about it.

I tried to ask for help. I tried to tell the doctors how I felt. My tongue refused to move. The doctors continued to beam at me.

'We'll let you get your rest now,' said Dr Bryce, 'and

when you wake up again, you can see your mum and dad.'

I closed my eyes. And, just like that, I was out of it.

For the next day I drifted in and out of myself. At least that's what it felt like. I don't remember too much about it. It just seemed that every time I opened my eyes, someone was smiling at me. Mum and Dad, the doctors, the nurses. I even dreamt that Trudy was smiling at me!

And then at last I opened my eyes and I was awake – really awake – and aware.

'How are we feeling, Cameron?' Dr Ehrlich was instantly at my side – smiling.

I coughed and instantly felt as if my chest was going to come apart.

'You will have a cough for a couple of days. That's the anaesthetic, I'm afraid. How's your throat?'

I swallowed hard. My mouth was no longer as dry as before. My throat wasn't as sore either - thank goodness.

'Better,' I croaked.

Was that really my voice? I sounded like a rusty frog!

'Would you like a little ice to suck on?'

'Yes, please.' I was still croaking.

The doctor used a teaspoon to fish a small chunk of ice out of the water jug on the table by my bed. She popped it into my grateful mouth. It was cool and wet and actually delicious.

'You are doing phenomenally well. You can sit up and, if the tests we run today are favourable, maybe we'll have you walking a couple of steps tomorrow.'

I stared at the doctor. She had to be kidding. I'd only just had a heart operation. What was going on? Were they short of beds or something?

'It's quite common practice.' The doctor's smile broadened. She could obviously read my expression. 'Not too long ago, it was standard practice to stay in bed for weeks after an operation. Now it's recognized that that's actually bad for you. We like to get our patients up and about as quickly as possible – even heart patients. D'you understand?'

I nodded, looking around. I took more of an interest in my surroundings. I wasn't in my room any more. There were machines all around me and I had an intravenous drip attached to each arm. Pads on my chest were hooked up to the heart monitor beside the bed. I had what looked like crocodile clips attached to the ends of two fingers and there was some kind of cuff around one of my ankles. I felt like Pinocchio before he had his strings cut! I looked up at the intravenous bags on either side of me. I pointed to the left one. 'What's in that?' I indicated with my head.

'It contains your anti-rejection drug,' said Dr Ehrlich.

'And that one?'

'Dextrose and saline.'

'Huh?'

'Sugar and salt water to make sure you don't become dehydrated.'

Dr Bryce entered the room. 'How are we feeling today?'

'Fine.' I shrugged. And I was feeling fine – in a peculiarly detached kind of way. Somehow it was all a bit of an anticlimax. I'd spent so many weeks thinking about the operation and the days leading up to it that I hadn't really given much thought to what would happen afterwards. And now here I was with not much of a clue as to what should or would happen next.

'We're amazed with your progress. You're doing extremely well,' Dr Bryce told me.

'Does that mean I can go home soon?' I asked.

There was no escaping the look that passed between Dr Bryce and Dr Ehrlich.

'Is something wrong?' I asked immediately.

'Nothing for you to worry about.' Dr Bryce's smile was as wide as it was false.

I studied him carefully. 'I thought you were going to be honest with me and not treat me like an idiot,' I said, disappointed.

Dr Bryce shook his head slowly. 'I'm sorry if that's how it came across. It's just that . . . we've had some bad news today – no, not about you or your operation,' he added quickly when he saw the look on my face. 'At least not directly.' The doctor paused, took a deep breath and turned to Dr Ehrlich. 'Janice, could you go and get Cameron's parents, please?'

'What's going on?' I struggled to sit further up in the bed. The bleep of the heart monitor was getting faster – as if I needed that to tell me that I was getting anxious. Mum and Dad came into the room, their expressions grim. Mum was carrying a newspaper. And in that instant I knew what had happened.

'I did ask all of you to keep this strictly confidential until I'd formally released the details to the media,' Dr Bryce said to no one in particular.

Which is how I knew that he knew it was me who'd let the cat out of the bag.

'Marlon gave me his word that he wouldn't tell anyone – not even his parents.' I couldn't deny that I'd been the one to blab but I still tried to defend myself.

'Well, this newspaper speaks for itself, doesn't it?' Mum said tersely.

Dad shook his head. 'I thought John and Erica were our friends.'

I thought of Marlon's mum and dad and all the times we'd been back and forth to each other's house. Our two families had even toured around the Lake District together.

'I'm sure that rag made them an offer they couldn't refuse,' Dr Bryce said with disgust.

'But they must've gone to the newspapers with the story to sell in the first place,' Mum pointed out.

DAILY PRESS

WORLD EXCLUSIVE!

THE BOY WITH A PIG'S HEART INSIDE HIS BODY!

TODAY THE DAILY PRESS CAN EXCLUSIVELY REVEAL THAT CAMERON KELSEY (ABOVE), AGED 14 OF LARKIN ROAD, DEALWORTH IN LONDON HAS MADE MEDICAL HISTORY.

In a dramatic twelve hour operation sure to send waves of controversy around the world, the heart of a pig has been transplanted into the body of Cameron Kelsey. With time running out for the sick child, and no likely prospect of a human donor, the only hope seemed to be eminent surgeon and immunologist Dr Richard Bryce. His pioneering techniques for overcoming rejection between species have opened the way for a new wave of transplants between animals and man.

Cameron Kelsey, the teenager from Dealworth, is remarkably cool about being a guinea pig on the frontiers of medicine. Asked about the special problems of using a pig-heart, he said, "It's simple really. The only thing I have to be careful about now is taking my medicine to stop my body rejecting my new heart." His mother Catherine said, "Cameron knows the risks, he knows that he faces a lifetime of check-

ups and anti-rejection drugs, but all he can talk about is going swimming and playing football." Cameron's heart was damaged beyond repair by a viral infection two years ago, and his life ever since has been a slow decline punctuated by major crises. "When Dr Bryce approached us, it was a shock, yes, but it was the chance for my son to lead a normal life. I leapt at the chance," said Mrs Kelsey.

Although the idea of transplantation from other species into humans has been discussed and debated for a few years now, this is the first time that such an operation has actually gone ahead. Dr Bryce has received media attention before when he first presented his opinion that the only way to overcome the shortage in human organs available for transplantation was to look at the organs of other species. No stranger to controversy, Dr Bryce has long sought to make his name – and his fortune – in this field.

Cameron Kelsey is known to be recovering in a private hospital and is thought to be doing well.

Friends close to the family told us that Cameron's parents allowed Cameron to make the final decision. After long and agonising deliberation, Cameron finally decided that he really had no other choice.

"It's simple really. I had to choose between living and dying – and I chose to live," said Cameron today. "And I'm feeling fine and fighting fit. I'd do the same thing again tomorrow!"

Cameron continued, "I can't wait to get back to school and start leading the life of a normal boy. I can't wait to swim and run and play football without getting breathless every two seconds."

Mrs Sola Shange, headmistress of Cameron's school, Ashmead Primary, said, "I knew that Cameron was in hospital for a transplant, but no, I didn't know...

continued on page 4

I stretched out my hand for the newspaper. Mum gave it to me without another word. Just one look at the headline was enough to confirm my worst fears.

'Cameron, you're to stay away from all of them – including Marlon, d'you hear me?' Mum fumed.

'This whole business will now be turned into a three-ringed circus.' Dr Bryce shook his head. 'And each of us will be considered exhibits.'

'Maybe it's just a one-week wonder,' Dad said hopefully. 'I'm sure the press will find something else to interest them tomorrow.'

Both Dr Bryce and Dr Ehrlich stared at Dad in stunned amazement. Mum just looked at him as if he'd lost his marbles. Me? I had other things on my mind.

Marlon was my best friend, and best friends didn't do that to each other. Friends didn't betray each other. Friends could keep secrets. I looked down at the newspaper again. The headline shrieked at me.

'I can't understand it,' I whispered. 'Why did Marlon do it? Why?' And at that moment, I felt more hurt inside than from anything the doctors had done to me over the last few days. Marlon was supposed to be my friend. In his shoes, I would never have told anyone. Never.

'Your friend's motives aren't the issue now. We all have to decide how to proceed from here. Mr and Mrs Kelsey, perhaps we could discuss this outside,' Dr Bryce suggested.

'No, this concerns me, doesn't it? This is about me,

isn't it? Shouldn't I be part of the discussion?'

Dad shook his head. 'We don't want you to be any more upset than you already are.'

'I couldn't be any more upset. But don't worry, I'm not about to keel over.'

Mum nodded slowly, then smiled.

'I don't think this is a very good idea . . .' Dad began.

Mum shrugged. 'Mike, as Cameron said, this does involve him too and if he feels up to it and Dr Bryce doesn't have any objections, I don't see why not.'

Dr Bryce took a good hard look at me and then visibly relaxed. 'Cameron, as I'm sure you'll appreciate, our first priority has to be to protect you. If we don't do something – and fast – the press will be all over your family like cheap perfume.' He sounded like he was quoting a line from one of those old black-and-white detective movies that Nan liked so much. It was so funny-peculiar to hear him say something like that that I almost smiled. Almost.

'So what do we do?' asked Mum.

'We spike their guns.' Dr Bryce replied without hesitation. 'I'll call an immediate press conference to tell the press exactly what's happened. Do you all have somewhere else to stay other than your house?'

Dad frowned. 'Why?'

'Because I think you should all lie low for a while – just until the hullabaloo has died down.'

'Lie low? We're not outlaws or criminals. Why should

we lie low?' Mum snapped out.

'Believe me, it's the best thing,' Dr Bryce soothed. 'It won't be for long. Just a month or two . . .'

'A month or two?' Mum wasn't the only one who was shocked.

'The press can be relentless.'

'No!' Mum's voice was quiet and all the more firm because of it. 'I'm not going to let the press – or anyone else for that matter – hound us out of our house. We haven't done anything wrong. I'm not going to let anyone treat us as if we have.'

'Mrs Kelsey, I really would recommend—'

'We are not moving out of our house and, just as soon as Cameron is fit enough, he's going back to school.' Mum's heels were well and truly dug in now.

'I'm sorry, Dr Bryce, but I think my wife is right. We'd have to face this sooner or later. Surely it's better to do it now and get it over with. Then we can all go back to normal,' said Dad.

'Mr and Mrs Kelsey, I think, no, I *know* you're under-estimating just what a pack of vultures you'll be dealing with. I've had the press camping out on my doorstep before. I know what I'm talking about,' Dr Bryce said sternly.

'As long as we have each other, we can handle it,' said Dad. 'It'll be a one-week wonder and then the whole thing will blow over.'

Mum looked up at Dad and smiled. For the first time

in a long time they smiled at each other and I was temporarily forgotten. But I didn't mind. To be honest, it was nice to see. It made a change.

'I think you're both deluding yourselves and for Cameron's sake I would urge you to reconsider.' Dr Bryce wasn't about to give up.

'We'll be OK.' Mum turned to smile at the doctor. 'The sooner we can get back to normal the better.'

The doctor shook his head. 'I'll call the press conference for tomorrow and another when Cameron is ready to go home.' He sighed. 'Are you both prepared to take part in the second conference with me?'

Dad turned to Mum, a questioning look on his face.

'Is that really necessary?' Mum asked.

'I would recommend it. It's better to throw the wolves a morsel or two than have them devour you alive, believe me,' Dr Bryce replied.

'Then we'll do it. Cameron is going to be fine and that's what I want to tell the world.'

'So when can I go home?' I asked Dr Bryce.

'If you carry on like this, I don't see any reason why you couldn't go home within the next month.'

'The next month!' I said, dismayed. 'That long?'

'Cameron, the worst thing I could do now is send you home before I'm one hundred percent convinced that the anti-rejection therapy is working. Don't forget, this particular type of transplant has never been done before.'

I slouched back against my pillows, disappointed. All I wanted to do now was go home, then go to school and show all my friends that I was the same as them. I wanted to play football and swim and dance. I smiled ruefully. I guess the truth of the matter was I wanted to show off. But until then, I'd just have to be patient.

Chapter Fourteen

The First Day

Hello, Alex.

How are you today? Me? I'm feeling fine. In fact I'm feeling super fine! I've never felt better. And yes, I am still in the hospital, but guess what? I'm going home tomorrow. Just a sec while I have a bop!

Not bad, huh! That's what Mum calls strutting my funky stuff! That's an oldie saying. I call it getting down with my bad self! And look! I danced around for ages and I'm not even out of breath. So this is what it's like to be healthy. I'd almost forgotten. It is so great to be fit! I feel as if I could run a marathon without even pausing to catch my breath. I've already packed my bags. It's been six weeks since my operation and I'm finally going home. It was beginning to feel as if Dr Bryce was never going to let me go. But today is the first day of the rest of my life.

The operation was a complete, utter and total success. Not only am I still standing but I'm running, jumping, dancing — you name it, I can do it. At last everything seems to be coming together. Mum and Dad are getting on much better now.

Mum's getting a bit of a tummy bulge now so I can see you growing. It's amazing. Mum says when she has her next scan, I can go with her so I can see what you look like inside her. Next time both Dad and I are going with her. I can't wait. D'you know how I feel now? Peaceful. I don't have a thing in the world to worry about. I really feel like I could live for ever.

Dr Bryce called his press conference. Mum and Dad wouldn't let me watch it on the telly. They said some of the reporters were bound to come up with really stupid questions and comments and they didn't want me to get upset. They watched it though. When I asked them how it went, all they said was – OK. I do wish they wouldn't treat me like a baby or, worse still, a cretin. Michelle, Pete and all the other nurses wouldn't tell me what happened at the press conference either. I'm meant to attend a press conference this Saturday with Mum and Dad. Mum reckons that once that's over, we'll have the media off our backs.

I'm still taking my anti-rejection medication. I have one injection a day. Dr Bryce says I'll have to keep giving myself these injections for the foreseeable future. The injections sting a bit but I don't mind. It was a bit daunting at first to have to stab myself with a needle but now I'm used to it. Diabetics have to do this sort of thing every day so it's not as if I'm alone. I probably won't be making quite so many of these recordings now. There's no point, is there? I'll be here when you arrive. I'll carry on until you are born though. I'll tell you things as they occur to me and as I live through them. It'll be a video diary from me to you.

Funnily enough, I eat much more healthily now than I did before the operation. I want to look after my new heart. I eat more salads and vegetables and fruit. And I don't eat red meat any more. Just fish and poultry. No particular reason. It's just healthier, that's all. I've decided to live until I'm 102. That's my lucky number – 102.

I'm looking forward to getting home and seeing most of my friends again. I haven't spoken to Marlon since I read the article in the Daily Press. *I know it was Marlon who told. No one else knew. More than once I picked up the phone to call him and ask him why, but then why should I? He should make the first move, not me. I know he can't phone me or come to see me because he doesn't know where I am, but let's just see what happens when I get home. He let me down.*

I might forgive him.

But I won't forget it.

Mum says Marlon's family got paid a load of money for the world exclusive they gave to that tabloid. Well, I hope Marlon enjoys the money.

I trusted him. It'll be a long time before I do that again.

Effect

Chapter Fifteen

The Arrival

One more road, one more corner and then we'd be
home. I knew it was silly to feel like this. Anyone would
think I'd never seen the place before, but it was *home*.
Tonight, I'd be sleeping in my own bed, in my own
bedroom.

'Cameron, stop bouncing up and down.' I caught
Dad's grin via the inside mirror. 'You're going to ruin
the car's suspension.'

'Aren't you glad to be home? Aren't you *excited*?' I
couldn't believe how cool Mum and Dad were acting.
For the last six weeks we'd all been living out of a
suitcase at Dr Bryce's clinic. I'd had more than enough
of that. Dr Ehrlich had dropped us all off at the nearest
mainline station, where Dad had his car waiting for us.
It'd been a long journey, with plenty of stops on the
way, but now *one more corner* . . .

'What on earth . . . ?'

I stared out of the windscreen at the crowds in front
of our house. It was like a crowd scene out of *Lord of the*

Rings. 'What's wrong with our house?' I asked anxiously.

I looked up past our house towards the sky. I couldn't see any smoke billowing, or flames pouring out of the windows. I could see a couple of police cars but no fire engines. Dad slowed down so that the car only crawled forward.

'Are you OK, Cathy?' he asked, his tone sombre.

Mum nodded. I could see them both tense up. It was only then that I realized what was going on. 'Are all those people waiting for *us*?' I asked, staggered.

Mum turned to me and nodded. 'When we get out, head straight for the front door and don't say a word to anyone. Leave the talking to your dad and me.'

'I want to know how all these people found out we'd be coming home today,' Dad said grimly.

'D'you think someone at the clinic told the papers?' Mum asked.

Dad shrugged. He didn't have time to say anything else. A couple of heads turned our way, then more and more. And then, what can only be described as a flood of people came rushing towards us. I shrank back in my seat, terrified. We were surrounded. There were people banging on the car and cameras covering every millimetre of the car windows. Questions were being shouted and screamed at us. There were men and women with microphones and notepads and digital-recorders as far as the eye could see.

'Don't stop the car, Mike,' Mum ordered.

'I have to. I can't get any closer to the house than this,' Dad replied.

I couldn't believe it. I stared at the crowd all around us, their mouths opening and closing, opening and closing. I'd once seen some sharks being fed and that's exactly what this was like. Only this time, Mum and Dad and I were the shark bait.

'Can we back up, Dad?' I asked.

But it was too late. The crowd had closed in behind us.

'CAMERON, CAN WE . . . ?'

'CAMERON, HOW DO YOU . . . ?'

'CAMERON, WHAT WILL YOU . . . ?'

The mob were banging on the car windows and firing questions at me from all directions.

'Mr and Mrs Kelsey?' Two policemen fought their way through the crowds to Dad's side of the car.

I'd never been so relieved to see anyone in my entire life.

'Yes,' Dad replied gratefully.

The policemen immediately turned to look at me. It took a few moments to decipher their expressions. Curiosity and something else. Not disgust exactly. More like . . . distaste? Distrust? Mentally I shook my head. I was imagining things. Seeing what wasn't there. More police turned up around the car, pushing back the crowds. The police formed a ring around us. One policeman who seemed to be in charge indicated that Dad should pull over.

It took Dad ages to drive the car the half a metre required to get to the pavement, what with the crowd pushing at the police and them shoving back. I'd never seen anything like it. When Dad finally did manage to park, we all sat still, each of us stunned. None of us was too keen to get out of the car – to say the least.

'Maybe we should have taken Dr Bryce's advice?' Dad ventured.

'No. This is our house,' said Mum. 'If we carry on as normal then everyone else will have to follow our lead. Besides, after the press conference tomorrow they'll all leave us alone.'

The chief policeman tapped on the driver's window. Dad wound down the window. 'Mr Kelsey? Mrs Kelsey? I'm Sergeant Dexter. If you and your family could get out of your car now, we'll escort you to your house.' The policeman was yelling over the noise of the crowd.

'Thank you. My wife is pregnant so could you please look after her?' Dad shouted back.

Sergeant Dexter nodded.

'Who phoned you, as a matter of interest?' Dad asked at the top of his voice.

'Dr Bryce warned us that you were on your way home and asked us to help. We sent one car but when we saw this lot, we had to call in reinforcements.'

Dad looked around at the braying crowd and shook

his head. He turned to Mum. 'Cathy, are you sure about this? Maybe we should stay in a hotel or with your mum for a while?'

'No.' Mum was adamant. 'This is our house. I want Cameron – and the rest of us – to get back to a normal environment as soon as possible.'

'I wouldn't call this normal.' Dad pointed at the crowd, still trying to swallow us up.

To be honest, I agreed with Dad. I'd had no idea it would be this bad. What did all these people want?

'OK then.' Dad sighed. 'Here goes.'

When Dad got out of the car, the decibel level rose perceptibly. I watched as he struggled past the police surrounding us to get to Mum's side of the car. He opened her door. I waited until Mum was out before opening my door and stepping out. The moment I set foot out of the car, the crowd erupted. From all sides people surged forward. The police had to link arms in a ring around us to stop them getting to us. I shrank back until the car was hard against my back. Mum and Dad stepped in front of me, but I could still see the faces. I could still hear them screaming at me.

'CAMERON, HOW D'YOU FEEL . . . ?'

'CAMERON, WHAT'S IT LIKE TO HAVE A PIG'S HEART . . . ?'

'WHY DID YOU DO IT . . . ?'

'HOW LONG WILL YOU LIVE NOW . . . ?'

'CAMERON . . . ?'

'CAMERON . . . ?'

On and on it went, on and on and on like a relentless tide. The police shifted to make a ring directly around us, excluding the car. And still the shouting and screaming and yelling and calling continued. There were TV cameras and camcorders all around. The police edged towards our house with us in the middle. When I'd seen movie stars or pop stars surrounded by their bodyguards and their fans on the telly before, I'd always thought that it must be fun to be famous. But if this was what it was like, then it was more terrifying than anything else. I looked around at the expressions on the faces of those immediately around us, beyond the police ring. They scrutinized me with rapt attention. Some of them were staring at me as if I'd just sprouted another head or something.

We moved up our garden path, through the heaving crowds, with the police and Dad yelling something about trespassing. And for the first time since my operation, I could hear my blood roaring in my ears. The roar was so loud it began to drown out the noise around me. Everyone and everything started to get swimmy and blurry.

I was going to faint.

No! NO! Not in front of these people, I told myself frantically. What would Mum and Dad say? What would my friends say? I'd never live it down. I took a deep breath, then another and another. We were close to the front door now. Dad struggled to get the front-door key in the lock. Intense lights blinked on and off all around us like mini lightning bolts. I turned my head slightly and was immediately blinded by more camera flashes. The front door opened.

Come on, Cameron. Breathe in. Breathe out.

The police ushered us into our house, with Sergeant Dexter and a policewoman leading the way. I'd barely got my feet on our doormat before the front door was shut behind me. The unbearable roar was turned into a bearable din outside the door. And my swimmy, sick feeling faded. In spite of the ringing phone we all stood in the hall like statues. No one said a word.

'Well, sir, welcome home!' said Sergeant Dexter drily.

Dad looked at him as if he was mad, then smiled slowly. 'Quite a homecoming,' he agreed. 'Are you all right, Cathy?'

Mum nodded. She headed for the ringing phone and picked it up. 'Hello?' she said.

I started to walk past her to go into the kitchen to get some water, but the changing expression on her face made me pause.

'No, we wouldn't be interested,' Mum said curtly. 'No . . . no, I'm afraid not. Goodbye.' She put the phone down. It immediately started ringing again. With a look of irritation, she picked it up. 'No, he won't,' she said after a pause. 'No. 'Bye.'

The moment the phone was down it started ringing

again. By now Mum's frown could've curdled milk. 'Hello?' There came a long pause as her frown grew deeper and deeper. 'No, we're not interested. Look, am I talking Martian? I said we're not interested . . . no . . . well, thank you very much. Goodbye!' She slammed the phone down. Without a second's pause it began to ring again.

'You're going to get that all day and all night, I'm afraid,' said the policewoman.

'Oh no, we won't,' said Mum. And she bent to pull the phone lead out of its socket.

We heard the sound of scuffles and then the doorbell rang. Through the frosted glass of the front door we saw the police usher some people away. I looked at Mum and Dad. I couldn't be the only one thinking that we were in a mad house in the middle of a nightmare.

'Cathy . . . ?'

'Let's wait until after the press conference, OK?' said Mum.

Dad smiled. Mum hadn't admitted that maybe she'd been wrong but it was close enough.

'Was it like this when you came back to get fresh clothes and that, after the story was in the papers?' I asked Mum and Dad.

I didn't miss the look that passed between them.

'A bit,' Dad admitted.

'Why didn't you tell me?'

'Because we both felt it would blow over.' Mum jumped in before Dad could answer.

'I don't know about blow over. Blow up, more like,' I said sourly.

'Don't let it worry you. And that goes for you as well, Cathy,' Dad said firmly. 'I'll take care of this business.'

I turned away just as Sergeant Dexter's walkie-talkie started beeping. I really hoped Mum was right and all this . . . chaos would disappear once the press conference was over.

'Right . . . right . . . OK . . . just a sec,' said Sergeant Dexter. He turned to me. 'We've got a boy outside who says he's your best friend. He says his name is Marlon Pearcy.'

Marlon . . .

'Should we let him in?' the sergeant asked patiently.

All eyes were on me as the sergeant waited for my answer. 'Mum told me not to speak to him,' I replied at last.

'No, Cameron, I shouldn't have done that. He's your friend and it's your decision, not mine,' said Mum.

And with those words I lost my ready-made excuse. I wanted to see Marlon. To be honest, I was desperate to talk to him. But all I kept seeing was the front page of the *Daily Press*. I couldn't seem to get past the fact that I had trusted Marlon and he'd let me down.

Slowly, I shook my head. 'I'm tired,' I lied. 'I'll see him on Monday at school.'

Sergeant Dexter spoke into his walkie-talkie. Mum and Dad watched me silently.

'I am tired,' I insisted.

'Of course,' Mum smiled. 'You take it easy. Tomorrow is going to be a long day.'

I ran upstairs to my room. I made it to the top of the stairs without having to pause for breath. And downstairs, I knew that Mum and Dad were watching me.

Chapter Sixteen

Questions

'If you could just put this microphone up your shirt and attach it there.'

I took the microphone from the woman who held it out and did as she'd asked. I couldn't get it attached though. Suddenly all my fingers had turned into thumbs.

She smiled. 'Here. Let me.'

Gratefully, I let her get on with it. She clipped the tiny microphone to one of my button holes. I wondered how powerful the microphone was. Would it be able to pick up my pounding heart? – 'cos that's what it was doing. Hammering. Pounding. Drumming like it was going out of fashion. And I had furious, charging elephants in my stomach. Mum and Dad were strangely quiet too. Dr Bryce and Dr Ehrlich chatted to each other as if they didn't have a care in the world. I envied them. They'd obviously done this many times before.

A short woman with blond hair tied back in a

pony-tail appeared in front of me from nowhere. She smiled at me. 'Just a touch of make-up.'

I drew away in horror. 'No, thank you.' What did she take me for?!

She smiled at the look on my face. 'It's just some powder to take the shine off your face while you're in front of the cameras. You don't want to shine like an oil slick, do you?'

'I don't mind,' I told her. 'I'm not an actor or anything. I don't need make-up.'

'I'll let you into a little secret,' she whispered. 'Footballers, boxers, sports stars in general; they all have make-up on when they're interviewed on the telly. That's what makes them look so good!'

'Footballers? Really?' I was still suspicious.

'Really!' The make-up lady nodded.

'Well, all right then,' I agreed reluctantly. 'But only powder. I don't want any mascara or lipstick or stuff like that.'

She laughed. ' 'Course not.'

Behind me I could hear Mum and Dad laughing too. I couldn't help flinching a bit when she dabbed at my face with a dry sponge covered in powder. The moment the press conference was over, I'd find the nearest sink and this muck was coming straight off.

I watched as she patted some powder on Mum's face and then Dad's. He looked about as impressed as I had been. Yeah, it wasn't so funny when he had to do it too! I looked around. My elephants were still charging.

'Mum, what if I say something wrong?' I whispered anxiously.

'You won't, dear.' Mum smiled. 'Just answer each question truthfully and then shut up.'

Dad started grinning. I frowned at Mum. If she thought she was putting my mind at ease, she was very much mistaken.

'The trick is to tell what you know, but don't tell all you know,' she continued.

Dad looked at her, surprised. 'What makes you such an expert?'

'I read it in a magazine somewhere,' she replied vaguely.

'Dr Bryce, aren't you nervous?' I interrupted his conversation with Dr Ehrlich.

'I'm always nervous at these things,' Dr Bryce admitted, to my surprise. He leaned closer and lowered his voice. 'But someone once told me that if you have to talk to a lot of people, just imagine them all naked and it makes you less nervous!'

I burst out laughing. 'Really?'

'Really!'

'Mr and Mrs Kelsey? Doctors? Cameron? We're ready for you now.'

A man wearing headphones with a microphone attached ushered us from the waiting room, then strode ahead to lead the way down the grey corridor. No one spoke. My mouth was so dry I wondered how I'd get out one word, never mind a sentence if anyone asked me anything. But hopefully all the questions would be directed at the doctors. I couldn't think what anyone would want to ask me – apart from how I was feeling. And that I could answer – just about.

We turned another corner, then came to a set of double doors with the large words QUIET PLEASE written on them. A red bulb was situated on the wall above the doors but it wasn't switched on. The man opened the double doors for us and we all trooped in, Dr Bryce first and me last. We were in a large studio with lots of huge lights hanging from the ceiling and at one end of the studio was a large table on a long platform. The table practically groaned under the weight of all the microphones that were on it. I'd never seen so many microphones in my entire life. And every light in the place seemed to be trained on the table. Rows of chairs were placed in front of the microphones, but they were in dark shadow. There was an aisle down the middle of the chairs and I could see a TV camero being pushed up it, closer to the table. Reporters and journalists sat on the chairs, with digital recorders and notepads. On either side of the chairs were yet more men and women with cameras. The cameras started flashing as soon as they became aware of our presence. Everyone stood up and turned to face us. An instant buzz filled the studio. Huge heavy studio cameras swung around to follow our progress.

I wanted to sit at the end of the table to be as inconspicuous as possible, but I was ushered to the chair next to Dr Bryce and he sat in the middle with the lights full on him. Glancing down the table, I saw Dr Ehrlich at one end of the table on the other side of Dr Bryce. Then there was me, and Mum and Dad sat at the other end of the table. As I looked around I felt like a rabbit caught in the headlights of a car. I sat in my chair, frozen. I couldn't have moved at that moment, even if the whole studio was on fire. It was like being in the car trying to get to our house all over again – except this was worse. I couldn't make out any faces – not full faces. They were shrouded in shadow. The intensely bright lights trained on our table were baking my head and making my skin prickle. If only the camera flashes would stop – just for a second.

'Quiet, please. Five seconds to air,' a man's voice yelled out from the floor before us.

Instantly the camera flashes stopped.

'Four . . . three . . .'

I looked around, panic-stricken. This was just a dress rehearsal, wasn't it? We would get the chance to hear the questions and practise first, wouldn't we?

A red light flashed on the TV camera directly in front of our table.

'I'd like to begin by reading a statement,' Dr Bryce immediately announced. He glanced down at a sheet of paper before looking into the huge TV camera ahead. 'For years now, the number of people waiting for heart transplants has far exceeded the number of hearts available for transplantation. At our research lab we've been working on ways to overcome this problem. Our solution has been to use the hearts of specially bred and genetically altered animals – in this case, pigs. Once government restrictions were lifted a few years ago, there was no reason why we couldn't proceed, confident of success. Cameron here is living proof that pig-heart transplantations do work. We've all been amazed at his progress. He's fitter and has a better quality of life now than he ever did. Cameron is our first success but I know he won't be our last. I think that at long last we can offer a viable remedy to those in urgent need of a heart transplant, who have been told time and time again that there are no hearts available. Thank you.'

As I watched the doctor deliver his speech, an icy feeling squeezed at my stomach and started to fan out through the rest of my body. He made the whole thing sound so cold, so clinical. He could've been talking about a new make of car that would make everyone's life better or a new brand of microwavable chip. Dr Bryce sat back, his hands on his lap, his fingers linked. I looked from his hands to his face and realized something. He was acting. I don't mean in an obvious, theatrical way. But his speech was well rehearsed and professionally delivered. And even his current pose was staged. I looked away, confused by my feelings. Why was I so . . . *disappointed*?

'Dr Bryce, how long did . . . ?'

'Dr Bryce, when did you first . . . ?'

'Dr Bryce, where did you . . . ?'

A tide of questions rushed towards us.

Dr Bryce smiled. 'One at a time, please.'

'Dr Bryce, how long was the operation?'

'Twelve hours.'

'Dr Bryce, d'you think it's ethically responsible to use the heart of a pig in a transplant operation?'

'Our pigs are specially selected, genetically altered and bred. We've spent many years and millions of pounds in research making sure that we are responsible. And if we hadn't performed the operation, then Cameron wouldn't be sitting here now,' Dr Bryce answered easily. 'Ask the millions of people around the world who are dying of heart disease whether or not they think heart transplants are a good idea. I'll let all those dying people do my talking for me.'

'But we're not talking about hearts donated by the loved ones of those who have died. We're talking about taking the heart of a domestic animal and putting it into a human,' another journalist stated.

'And if the heart works and prolongs life?' asked Dr Bryce.

'Is that your only consideration?' asked yet another journalist.

'As a doctor, it's my sworn duty to improve the quality of life. I'm not going to apologize for that.'

'Don't you think you're behaving like Dr Frankenstein and creating monsters?'

'Are you calling me a monster?' I got in before Dr Bryce could.

The woman who'd asked the question turned to me. 'I didn't mean to imply that you're a monster as such. But how do you feel, knowing that a pig's heart is beating inside your body?'

'It's just a heart. A muscle. It has nothing to do with what I am or how I think or behave or feel,' I replied.

'Did Dr Bryce tell you to say that?'

'Dr Bryce doesn't have to tell me what to say,' I said, annoyed. 'I've got a brain of my own and a mouth of my own. I'm not some kind of ventriloquist's dummy with his hand up my jumper!'

'Cameron . . .' Mum nudged me and mouthed the warning.

'But, Mum, they keep asking stupid questions,' I protested. The only trouble was, I'd forgotten about the microphone attached to my shirt and my voice boomed out around the studio. 'Sorry,' I quickly mumbled.

I bent my head, hoping and praying that this was just a dress rehearsal. Something told me that it wasn't though. 'Cameron, how are you feeling?'

'Fine, thank you.' From now on, I'd keep my answers short and sweet.

154

'Mr and Mrs Kelsey, what do you say to all those people who'll accuse you of allowing your son to be used as a guinea-pig?' asked someone else.

I looked down at my lap at this point, remembering that those were the exact some words Mum had used when Dad first told us about Dr Bryce.

'Anyone who has a child who is ill with heart disease will know what all of us were going through,' said Mum. 'Our son was very ill. He only had a few more months to live. This was a chance at life and he wanted to grab it with both hands. Neither his father nor I could or would stand in his way under those circumstances.'

'Mrs Kelsey, do you believe you did the right thing in allowing the operation to go forward?'

'Yes, I do,' Mum said at once. 'It's what Cameron wanted and that's all that mattered.'

'And would you do the same thing again?'

'Under the same circumstances – yes, of course,' Mum replied without hesitation.

'And you, Cameron? Any regrets?'

'Like Dr Bryce said, I wouldn't be here now if it wasn't for the operation,' I said.

No, I wouldn't be here now. I'd be at home lying in bed or reading or playing on the computer – just passing the time until there was no more time to pass.

'Do you feel any different, Cameron?'

'No. Not at all. Just fitter.'

155

'Will your son be returning to school, Mrs Kelsey?'

'Yes, on Monday.'

'Do you consider him to be a normal boy now?'

'How else would I consider him?' Mum replied tersely.

'Cameron, what about your friends? How have they taken to your new heart?'

'I haven't seen any of them since my operation,' I admitted.

'Dr Bryce . . . ?'

'Dr Ehrlich . . . ?'

'Mr and Mrs Kelsey . . . ?'

'Cameron . . . ? Cameron . . . ? Cameron . . . ?'

On and on and on they went, until my head was buzzing with question after question.

'Mum?' I whispered.

Mum bent her head so that her ear was next to my mouth.

'Mum, I don't want to answer any more questions.' I made sure my voice was no more than a murmur so that the microphone wouldn't pick it up.

'Are you tired?' she asked, immediately concerned.

After a moment's pause, I nodded.

'Excuse me, everyone, but my son is getting tired so I'm afraid we'll have to leave now.'

'Cameron, are you feeling ill . . . ?'

'Just one more question . . .'

'One more question, Cameron . . .'

A number of the reporters had risen to their feet now. The lights were making me feel hot and sick. I desperately wanted to leave.

Mum stood up, a steely look on her face. I knew that look and for once I was glad of it. Mum was leaving and nothing and no one could stop her. Dad stood up and put his arm around her before helping her, then me off the raised platform where we sat. I could hear the murmurs of disapproval and protest as we left the table.

'Ladies and gendemen, Dr Ehrlich and I will be more than happy to answer any further questions you may have,' Dr Bryce soothed. 'And I have a very important announcement to make. Today I can formally announce that my clinic's next xenotransplant will take place next week.' Everyone was on their feet shouting questions at that, but I let it wash over me. The man who had ushered us to the table appeared to show us across the studio to the exit. As we walked past the chairs, I risked a glance at the reporters. It was feeding time at the zoo again. They were devouring me with their eyes. A man pushed forward and stuffed a white envelope into my hand. Another woman knocked over her chair in her effort to get to me. She handed me a large brown envelope. I frowned down at the letters in my hand. What was all this about? And then we were outside the studio. The air felt cooler. I leaned against the wall and took several relieved deep breaths.

'Thank you for attending the press conference.' The

man with the headset shook Mum and Dad's hands. 'I'll just retrieve your mikes.' I unclipped the mike, pulled it out from under my shirt and handed it back to him. He smiled at me. 'You did very well, Cameron.'

I didn't answer.

'Anyway, take care and good luck to all of you. Take the lift over there down to the ground floor. The receptionist will make sure the car is here to take you home.'

'Thanks,' Dad replied.

'Is that it, Dad?' I asked. 'D'you think they'll leave us alone now?'

Mum and Dad looked at each other.

'Let's hope so, Cameron,' Dad replied grimly. 'Let's hope so.'

Chapter Seventeen

Offers

When we finally got home, I have to admit, I was dog-tired. I put it down to the anxiety of going on the telly for the first time – and the last, if I had my way. There was still a crowd outside our house: it wasn't as big as the day before, but it was big enough. My heart sank at the prospect of us having to fight our way through yet more people. Luckily there were also two policemen I hadn't seen before near our house. They made a bee-line for us.

'Am I glad to see you! How come you're still here?' asked Dad.

'Sergeant Dexter thought a couple of us had better stay here to make sure the crowd behaves,' said one of the policemen.

We were escorted through the crowd into our house. On the way a woman shouted out to me, 'Can I shake your hand, Cameron?'

I was so surprised that a perfect stranger should want to shake my grubby hand that I actually put it out. Only then did I realize I was still holding the two envelopes

I'd been given at the TV studio. I'd forgotten all about them. I switched them to my other hand.

The woman beamed at me. 'Good luck!'

I smiled back, unsure of what to say. We entered our house. The police stayed outside.

'Cathy, would you like a cup of peppermint tea?' Dad asked.

'Yes, please.' Mum sighed gratefully. 'What a day!'

'I'll massage your feet as well if you like,' said Dad.

Rather him than me! 'What about my feet?' I asked.

'Your cheesy feet! You must be joking. You've got two hands, haven't you?' said Dad. 'Get on with it!'

So that was that! Not that I'd expected anything else. I tore open the first envelope, wondering what was so important. I started to read, and the more I read the more amazed I became. I literally couldn't believe my eyes. I read it again, thinking that maybe someone was playing a joke on us.

'Cam, what's the matter?' asked Mum.

Stunned, I looked up at her. I handed her the letter without a word. Mum's expression mirrored my own as she started to read.

'My eyes aren't playing tricks on me, are they?' I whispered.

'What's going on?' Dad asked.

'This newspaper is offering us thousands of pounds for our story.' Mum handed Dad the letter. 'They want our exclusive story and unlimited access to Cameron for the next year.'

As Dad read the letter, I tore open the second letter that had been thrust into my hands.

'Yes!' I squealed with delight. 'We're rich! This news-paper is offering even more money than the first one.'

Mum snatched the letter out of my hand. I started dancing around the hall. 'We're rich! We're rich! I can get a mountain bike with twenty-four gears! I could get a *car* if I wanted to.'

A slow, burning frown crept over Mum's face. Dad stared at me.

'What's the matter?' I asked.

Anyone would think the roof had just blown off rather than not one but two offers of tons of money in the very same day. Mum and Dad looked at each other. Without saying a word, they both proceeded to tear each offer into shreds.

'What're you doing? Are you mad?' I stared at the bits of paper Mum was piling into Dad's cupped hands. I followed Dad as he walked into the living room and dumped the whole lot into the wastepaper bin. I fell to my knees and scrambled in the bin to fish the pieces out again.

'Cameron, get up. Now.' Dad used a tone of voice that I'd never heard before. It stopped me cold. I looked up at him. His eyes were sparking with anger. Anger directed solely at me. 'Get off your knees.'

I stood up, although I could hardly drag my eyes away from the bin. 'But, Dad, that's a lot of money.'

'I don't care if they offer ten times as much, my answer would still be the same. I'm not letting the papers or the telly or anyone else into our lives like that.'

'But . . . but . . . I don't understand.'

'Cameron, your dad and I want this family to get back to normal as soon as possible,' said Mum. 'We want our lives to get back to the way they were — private and ours. We can hardly say we want our privacy if we let a tabloid plaster our faces and our whole lives over its front page, now can we?'

'But what about all that money?' I couldn't believe that Mum and Dad would pass up on opportunity like this. 'They're going to pay us a fortune.'

'Not if we say no, they're not,' said Mum.

'But you can't say no. You just can't. We could have a new house and a new car and anything we want.'

'We have a roof over our heads, bread on the table and each other. What more do we want?' Dad smiled.

'I'm being serious.' I was practically shouting by now. I couldn't help it. All that money had danced in front of me and now, because of Mum and Dad, it was dancing away out of reach. 'If we don't take the money, they'll just give it to the next transplant patient Dr Bryce talked about. That's our money.'

Dad's smile disappeared. 'That is not our money,

162

Cameron. The press aren't getting our story 'cos we have nothing to tell them.'

'They want my story, not yours. You don't have a story.' Fury sat like a boulder on my chest. 'By rights that's my money, not yours. You've got no right to say no. I want—'

'Cameron, that's enough.' Mum frowned. 'We said no, and that's final.'

'I hate you. I hate both of you,' I shouted.

And I ran up the stairs to my bedroom as fast as I could. I didn't stop until I threw myself on the bed, every part of my body clenched and angry. I waited to hear footsteps climbing the stairs. At any moment now Mum and Dad would come into my room and tell me that if I really wanted to give my story to the papers, they'd let me do it. Any second now . . .

But there were no footsteps. My bedroom door didn't open. I sat up on my bed and watched the door. Dr Bryce had given me a new lease of life and, just like that, Mum and Dad were determined to ruin it. Images of money swirled around me. Notes, up to the ceiling. Five- and ten- and twenty- and fifty-pound notes spread out as far as the eye could see, and it could've all been mine.

How could they? I would never, ever forgive them. Not if I lived to be 150.

'Cameron, come on downstairs for your dinner.' Mum popped her head around my door.

'I'm not hungry.' I didn't look up from my book.

I'd been in my bedroom for over two hours now and I had no intention of coming out for the rest of the night. I sensed rather than saw Mum come over and sit on the bottom of my bed.

'Did you speak to Alex today?' Mum asked me unexpectedly.

'No.' I looked at her. 'Why?'

'I think you should,' said Mum. 'I think you should tell Alex exactly what's going on.'

'I don't need to any more.' I frowned. 'I'm going to be around for a good while yet.'

'I know. But you can still tell Alex all about the months before he or she is born.'

'I thought that but then I thought maybe it was tempting fate,' I said doubtfully.

'A lot of things are going to happen to all of us in the next few months. Some good. Some bad. You'll never have another opportunity like this to let Alex know what's going on in our lives. I think you'll kick yourself if you miss this chance.'

'I . . . I'll think about it,' I replied.

Mum smiled. 'Fine.' She stood up and walked to the door. 'I'll keep your dinner in the oven for you, just in case you change your mind.'

'I won't.'

'We'll see,' was all she said.

'Mum, I'm sorry I said I hated you and Dad,' I mumbled. 'I didn't mean it.'

'I know. But that's why you have to be careful about money.'

'Money being the root of all evil,' I supplied dismissively. The last thing I wanted from Mum was a morality lecture.

'Money can do a lot of good things. Money isn't the root of all evil. *Love* of money is the root of all evil,' Mum amended. 'You think about what happened when we told you we were going to turn down those offers made by the newspapers. You turned into someone else – someone I could barely recognize. You'll have to watch that, Cameron. Hold on to the things that mattered before your operation.'

I frowned at Mum. I hadn't a clue what she was talking about.

'Cameron, you're a very special boy. Your dad and I love you very much – we always have and we always will. But now lots of people are going to say you're only special because of your operation. They'll want to throw money at you and goodness only knows what else. But don't let them, or you'll start to believe that the only thing about you that's worth anything is your new heart. And then the true you will get lost. D'you understand?'

I shook my head.

'Never mind. Maybe one day you will. See you

downstairs,' Mum said. And she shut the door behind her.

I felt really strange once Mum had left. I stood up and walked over to my dressing table. Staring at myself in the mirror, I replayed in my head everything that had happened downstairs. Everything I'd said, everything I'd done. I thought over what Mum had just said, grasping to understand what she'd tried to tell me. But the more I thought about it, the more confused I felt. I took the camcorder bag out from under my bed.

Hi, Alex,

It's me again. We've just come back from a press conference. My first and last, I hope. Dr Bryce didn't put a foot wrong. I didn't put a foot right. Dr Bryce talked about me as if I was just a piece of machinery on an assembly line.

The first of many. Bring them on. Next!

That's how I felt when he was talking. But then, what did I expect? I don't know. Maybe I expected him to refer to me more. Maybe I expected him to refer to me less. Maybe I wanted to be special, unique. I don't know. All I know is, it was hot and bright under the lights and after a while I began to feel very sick. I was glad to get out of there. On the way out, two journalists stuffed envelopes into my hand. And guess what? Two newspapers offered me thousands and thousands for my story.

Me! Can you imagine?

But Mum and Dad said no and put the letters in the bin. I hit the roof. I mean, I went absolutely ballistic. All I could see was the money I was losing. It was as if they were stealing it out of my pocket — which of course they weren't. I can't believe how I blew up at them. I mean, I still don't see why we can't just take the money, give the papers a couple of interviews and laugh all the way to the bank, but I shouldn't have lost my temper like that. I don't know what came over me.

Yes, I do.

I think I became blinded by the pound signs in my eyes. It was a lot of money. Ah well! At least one day I'll be able to look back and say I was offered a fortune for my life story. Me! There's not many people who can say that!

I think I'll shut up now. I'm hungry. I'm going to go down for my dinner.

Talk to you soon!

'Mum, where's my dinner?'

Mum and Dad exchanged a smile.

'In the oven. Hungry now?'

'Starving.'

'Are you going to eat it with us?' asked Dad.

I frowned. 'Where else would I eat it?'

'Just wondered,' Dad said in a fake off-hand manner.

'Sorry about earlier,' I mumbled, and sat down.

'Your dinner's in the oven,' Mum repeated pointedly.

'Oh! And I'm big enough and ugly enough to get it myself, eh?' I stood up again.

Mum and Dad laughed. 'You said that,' said Dad. 'We didn't!'

Chapter Eighteen

School

It was early Monday morning and we still had a crowd outside our house – although it seemed that Mum was right: the crowd was dwindling. Mind you, they still weren't disappearing fast enough for my liking.

'Am I going to have to walk through that lot to get to school?' I said, frowning out of the front-room window.

'No. Until this whole thing blows over, your dad or I will take you to school,' said Mum.

'But Dad's gone to work.'

'So I'll drive you today.'

'You'll drive me?'

'Yes. I can drive, you know. I have passed my test.'

'But that was when you had to crank up the engine from the front of the car to start it!' I scoffed. 'And you hate driving!'

'Well, I'll just have to learn to love it, won't I? The police have recommended that that's what we do until all those people outside our house get a life.' Mum sighed.

'But why go to all this bother?'

Mum looked away from me. She couldn't meet my eyes and, in that instant, I knew that something was very wrong.

'Mum . . . ?'

'Come on, we'd better get going. You don't want to be late on your first day back at school.'

I watched Mum but I didn't say anything. This was totally unlike her. Mum believed in straight talk and no nonsense. Say what you mean and mean what you say, that was her motto. She was the last one to hide anything from me but that's what was happening.

'Won't some of these journalists and rubber-neckers be at school too?' I asked.

'They have to stay outside the school grounds or they'll be arrested. Journalists have to get school and local authority permission before they can go onto the school premises,' Mum told me. 'In fact, you'll probably get more privacy at school than in this house.'

Silence.

'Are you all right, Mum?'

'I'm fine.'

'What about Alex?'

Mum patted her pregnant bulge. 'Alex is fine too. You've given yourself your anti-rejection injection?'

'Yes, Mum. And I've taken my tablets and my medicine.' Mum asked me that question every morning without fail.

169

'Then we'd better go. Are you ready, Cam?'

I nodded. Something was going on. The question was what? I didn't ask and Mum wasn't going to say but I was determined to find out.

'Cameron, how are you?'

'How are you feeling?'

'We saw you on the telly!'

From the moment I walked into school I was surrounded by my friends and others who'd never had one word to say to me before. Although it was embarrassing, in a strange way it was also quite nice! I was the centre of attention. I was *special*. A couple of kids even asked me for my autograph. It was bizarre!

'I saw you on telly, weed!' Travis pushed his way through the crowd to stand in front of me. 'I was surprised you had the guts.'

'My name is Cameron, not weed,' I told him. 'And I've got guts and a lot more besides. Now, could you shift, you're in my way.'

Travis looked around. 'Well, you're braver than me.' I stared at him. That was the very last thing I'd expected him to say. 'I don't know if I could've done what you did,' he continued.

'You couldn't, muscle-head!' I told him without hesitation. 'Excuse me.' I swept past him in the best royal fashion. The monarchy would've been proud of me! If Travis thought we could be friends now, he had another thought coming. Not after all the grief he'd given me over the last year!

I didn't so much walk as allow myself to be swept along to class by the crowd of people around me. And then I saw him – Marlon. I stopped and we both just looked at each other. I didn't know what to say or do – so I said and did nothing. I walked past him without a word. Even as I was doing it, I wanted to stop and go back and say sorry and laugh and have everything just as it'd been before. But then I was angry with myself. Why should I apologize? He was the one who should say sorry, not me! And I had the image of the front page of the *Daily Press* in my head to prove it. So why was I so upset?

By the time Mr Stewart arrived I had so many people around me, I couldn't move.

'Anyone who's not in my class can leave – NOW!' Mr Stewart bellowed out.

To be honest, I was glad to see him. All those people surrounding me and asking question after question made me feel as if I was being pecked to bits. Without ceremony, Mr Stewart ushered out all those who shouldn't have been in his class.

The noise was deafening – chatter and laughter and a couple of prods in the back from Andrew, who sat behind me. I grinned at him and looked around, glad to be back. There was Julie. She caught me watching her and immediately looked away. Now that I was like everyone else, maybe Julie and I . . . My face burning, I carried on looking around. I didn't want anyone else to look at me and guess what I was thinking. Marlon stood over by the window, watching me. I hadn't seen him standing there when I'd been surrounded. He waited until the rest of us had sat down at our desks before coming over to sit next to me.

'Cameron, can I talk to you?' he whispered.

I looked directly at him. 'What about?'

'I . . . I'm sorry about the newspaper article . . .'

'Is that all you've got to say? You're sorry?'

Neither of us spoke above a fervent whisper. Mr Stewart was still chucking kids out of his class, but I didn't want to attract his attention – or anyone else's, for that matter.

'What d'you want me to say?' Marlon asked.

'You promised me you wouldn't tell anyone about my operation. Now we can't get out of the house for the crowds. We can't use our phone 'cos we've got people calling us day and night. We can't even pick our noses in peace without our every movement being recorded and analysed. We have to keep all the upstairs curtains drawn to stop reporters trying to spy in from our neighbours' houses. And we have you to thank for all of that.'

'You don't understand. I was upset about . . . about what might happen to you. Mum kept pestering me until I told her why I was moping around the house. I

172

made her promise not to tell anyone, but she told Dad and he was the one who told the newspapers.'

'I hear your family made a lot of money from selling me out.' I was scornful.

'It wasn't me,' Marlon protested. 'Dad did it, not me.'

'Excuse me, but I told you and only you. And I told you to keep it a secret. Don't blame your dad because he can't keep his mouth shut either. If you'd kept your promise, your dad would never have had a story to tell – or sell.'

'I'm sorry. I'm sorry. *I'm sorry!* What more can I say? It won't happen again – I promise.'

'Too right it won't happen again.' My eyes narrowed as I regarded Marlon. 'You must be nuts if you think I'd ever trust you with another secret.'

'You *can* trust me. I won't let you down again . . .'

'Read my lips. You won't get the chance. D'you get it? D'you dig it? D'you *grab*?!'

'Er . . . that's enough talking, thank you,' Mr Stewart hollered. 'What is the matter with everyone today? It's just your ordinary, everyday, standard Monday morning, so let's get on with it.' He looked at me.

Please don't ask me to say a few words, I prayed. Please don't.

'Welcome back, Cameron.' Mr Stewart smiled. 'Now then, while I take the register you can all get out your maths books. Double maths first thing on a Monday morning. I love it!'

I smiled my thanks at Mr Stewart. Thank goodness he hadn't asked me to show myself up.

'Here, Cam.' Andrew prodded me in the back again. 'We're going swimming tomorrow afternoon after school. D'you want to come?'

'Yeah, all right. Er . . . I'll have to check and make sure it's OK first,' I amended.

Now that I was well, I wouldn't have to bend the truth any more about where I was going each Tuesday evening. I'd ask Mum and Dad if it was OK for me to go swimming. I was sure they'd say yes. Dr Bryce had said I could do anything I wanted, I just shouldn't overdo it. My body needed time to build in strength and stamina after two years of no exercise because my old heart couldn't take it. But now I had a new heart in me. That thought never ceased to amaze me. I took my pulse. It was strong and regular just the way it should be.

'Are you OK?' Marlon asked immediately.

I frowned. 'Yes. Why wouldn't I be?'

'You're taking your pulse.'

'So? I'm fine. Or are you looking for more info to sell to the papers?'

The moment the words were out I was sorry. I opened my mouth to say so but Marlon had turned away and the moment was lost. I didn't know what was wrong with me. I seemed to be lashing out – there was no other way to describe it – and I had no idea why. First Mum and Dad, then Travis, now Marlon.

'If I was the one who'd had a heart transplant operation and you were the one who'd told, I would've forgiven you,' Marlon said quietly.

I looked at him. He looked straight ahead at the teacher.

'I have forgiven you,' I said.

'No, you haven't,' Marlon replied.

'Yes, I have.'

Marlon looked at me. He just looked. And in that moment, I knew and he knew that I was lying. He was right. In spite of all the things I told myself about forgiving but not forgetting, I knew that I hadn't forgiven Marlon. Deep inside, I was still angry. Deep inside, I was still hurt.

For the rest of the double lesson Marlon and I listened to Mr Stewart drone on and did the exercises we were meant to in our maths books. But we didn't say a word to each other. That was something that had never happened before. And I didn't like it.

Chapter Nineteen

The Right Moment

When the double lesson was over, I made a bee-line for Julie's desk. I wanted to get to her before she left the classroom. If she was surrounded by all her friends, I'd never pluck up the courage to do this. As she looked up, I gave her what I hoped was my best smile. She got the teeth and all! Julie looked away, her expression serious. I wondered if she knew what was coming. Or had I done something to upset her? No, I couldn't have. I'd only just got back to school, for goodness' sake.

Get a grip, Cam! I told myself sternly.

It was now or never. I took a deep breath and forced myself to speak before I could chicken out. 'Hi, Julie.'

'Oh, hi, Cameron . . .' There was a distinctly frosty look on Julie's face. And it wasn't getting better, it was getting worse.

'How are you?' I asked to fill the uncomfortable silence descending between us.

Julie started reading the book in front of her. I might've thought she didn't want to speak to me if it hadn't been for the fact that the book was upside down and it took Julie several seconds to realize it.

I smiled. 'You might find this easier.' And I picked up her book and turned it round for her. When I handed it back to her, she drew away as if I was about to slap her. My smile faded. 'What's the matter?' I asked.

'Nothing.'

'Here you are.' I tried to give back her book. She drew away even further. 'Is something wrong?' I asked.

'Just leave it on my desk.' Julie tried for a smile, but it came nowhere near her eyes.

Puzzled, I regarded her. I had no idea what I'd done, but I'd obviously done something. Was she upset because I hadn't told her all about my operation? I hadn't told anyone all the facts, except Marlon. I couldn't believe she wasn't talking to me because of that.

'What're you reading anyway?' This wasn't going as well as I'd hoped I was looking for the right moment to invite Julie to the pictures, but the right moment was rapidly disappearing over the horizon. I looked at the cover of the book Julie had been reading. It was a book called *Computer Ghost* by some woman I'd never heard of before. The cover was good though. A whirling, swirling mist surrounding a computer screen.

'Can I borrow it after you?' I asked.

'You can take it now if you like,' Julie said quickly.

'But you haven't finished it . . .'

'Yes, I have. I've already read it. I was just reading it again. Go on, take it.'

And as I looked at Julie, it slowly dawned on me what was going on. She was *scared* of me. I couldn't believe it and yet . . . and yet I was sure I was right.

'I don't bite, you know.' I tried to say it as a joke, but I couldn't keep the edge out of my voice. I thrust the book back at Julie.

She took a deep breath. 'Look, Cam, I'm not being funny but Mum said you could have all kinds of germs and diseases in you now. Germs and diseases that are new to humans and dangerous. Mum said I wasn't to go anywhere near you.'

It was as if Julie had kicked me in the stomach. I was only vaguely aware of the stillness rippling through the classroom. I stared at Julie. She frowned at me.

'I don't want to be mean, but you wouldn't take the hint,' she whispered.

'Julie, it's still me – inside and out. I haven't changed.'

'You've got a pig's heart inside you. Of course you've changed,' Julie said, her voice fearful – and angry because of it.

'I haven't got any germs or diseases,' I protested. My mouth felt as if it was filled with ashes and they were choking me.

'You don't know that. Not for sure. My mum said . . .'

'I don't give a stuff what your mum said. What do you say?' I asked.

'Cameron, can we just leave it?' Julie looked around the classroom, embarrassed. I didn't take my eyes off her.

'What do *you* say?' I asked again.

It was like having a sore tooth that you keep prodding with your tongue even though it hurts, or a scab you keep picking. I knew I should walk away. I knew I should just leave, but I had to hear her say it.

'I think Mum's right. You've got a pig's heart inside you, so how d'you know what's going on in your body now?'

Slowly, I put the book back down on Julie's desk. I looked around the classroom. Some people couldn't meet my eyes ond they looked away. Others looked straight back at me. I realized that Julie wasn't alone. Some of the others didn't like the idea of being near me either. I'd been so blinded by all the people surrounding me earlier that I hadn't noticed the ones who kept well away.

I looked down at the ground. I couldn't bear to catch anyone else's eye. Turning, I left the classroom, quietly shutting the door behind me.

Chapter Twenty

Nan

'How was school today?' Mum asked.

School was over and we were driving back home. I sighed and looked out of the windscreen. 'Complicated,' I replied at last.

'Ah!' Mum didn't say anything else and she didn't ask why.

To be honest, for once I wouldn't have minded if she had asked me to explain. On the way home I tried a couple of times to tell her what Julie had said. More than once I tried to tell her about me and Marlon, but the right moment and the right words never really presented themselves.

When we got home, there was a crowd of only about twenty people. A definite improvement.

At the expression on my face, Mum said, 'Yes, I know! By the end of the week let's hope they'll all be gone.'

With a policewoman's help we managed to reach our house without too much pushing and shoving. At least on this front, things were getting better. I walked into the living room, where I got a wonderful surprise.

'Nan!'

'Cameron, you goose! How are you?'

Nan threw down the magazine she was reading, sprang off the sofa and gave me a big hug. I was so pleased to see her that I let her!

'So what's all this about you having a pig's innards in your chest?' Nan thumped the back of her hand against my chest. 'And why do I have to buy the *Daily Press* to find out what's going on with my own grandson?'

'We told you Cam was going to have a heart transplant,' Mum tried.

'You didn't say where the heart was coming from though, did you?'

Mum sighed. 'I've been getting grief for that all day.'

I made the big mistake of trying to explain. 'Nan, we couldn't tell anyone. Dr Bryce told us not to.'

'And just when did I become – anyone! I'm your nan – not *anyone*.'

'Mother, don't start again. *Please*,' Mum pleaded. 'And we did phone you as soon as the story hit the newspapers.'

'Hhumph!' Nan sniffed. 'It was a little late by then, don't you think?' When Mum looked suitably contrite, Nan softened a little. A very little. 'Anyway, I saw all of you on the telly and I saw the crowds outside your house. You obviously need me here.'

'With you here, we don't need the police,' I murmured.

Nan smiled. 'Thank you, Cameron – I think!'

I'd forgotten she had ears like a bat! And eyes like a spy satellite. Not much got past my nan. She was looking more tired than the last time I'd seen her though. I looked at her, really looked at her, and for the first time she appeared . . . old. She seemed smaller, more fragile. Her shoulders dropped and even when she smiled it was as if a sigh wasn't too far away.

Mum moved over to the sofa and picked up Nan's magazine. I saw her shake her head. She held it up behind Nan's back for me to see. It was a magazine about coffins!

'Nan, why're you reading that?' I asked, pointing to it with distaste.

Nan turned to see what I was talking about. 'Cam, I'm no spring chicken any more and I have to think about these things. I'm going to be in my coffin a long time, so I want to make sure I pick out one that's comfortable.'

Mum shook her head even more at that. I know I should've been used to Nan by now but I still thought the idea was really morbid.

'Right! Well, I'll leave you two to it. I'm off to do some food shopping,' said Mum, leaving the room. 'I think we'll see about getting our phone number

182

changed as well, seeing as how our number has been leaked to the press.'

Nan took my arm and we went over to the window. 'Your fan club?' she said drily. 'You should attach a garden hose to the cold tap in the bathroom and let them all have it!'

'OK, Mum. Drive safely. 'Bye, Mum!' From the hall, Mum called out all the things I suppose I should've said to her.

' 'Bye, Mum,' I called back.

'Huh!' Mum guffawed.

She retrieved her car keys from the hall table and I heard our front door open and close. Nan sat down on the sofa, then patted the space next to her. I sat down eagerly.

'So, how're you doing?' she asked without preamble.

'Fine, I guess,' I answered lightly.

Nan gave me a look. 'This is your nan you're talking to, not your mum and dad. I'll ask you again, how're you doing?'

I sighed and slumped right back on the sofa. 'I suppose I'm all right. I've never been healthier. I've never felt so fit . . .'

'But?'

'But suddenly everything seems so complicated,' I admitted.

'In what way?'

'Did Mum tell you we were offered a lot of money for our story?'

'Yes.'

'What do you think of that?'

'I think your mum and dad should take the money and run. If the papers are stupid enough to offer that kind of money then I would grab it with both hands. But I appreciate your mum's reasons.'

'They were offering a whole lot of money.' I couldn't keep the wistful note out of my voice.

'That's 'cos they have more money than sense,' Nan said scathingly.

We sat in silence for a while, but it wasn't an uneasy silence. Nan knew there was more coming. She was just letting me tell it in my own time.

'Dr Bryce made us promise not to tell anyone about the operation,' I began at last. 'Not even you, although Mum and Dad wanted to. The only thing we could tell anyone was that I was having a heart transplant. We couldn't say where the heart was coming from. But . . . but I told my best friend, Marlon. He promised me he wouldn't tell anyone else, but . . .'

'But that's how it got into the papers?'

I nodded. 'Marlon says his dad told the papers, but then Marlon shouldn't have blabbed it to his mum and dad in the first place.'

'You mean, the way you shouldn't have blabbed it to Marlon in the first place?' Nan asked.

'That's different,' I said at once.

'How so?'

'It was my secret to tell,' I said, annoyed. 'It wasn't Marlon's.'

'True.'

'There! I knew you'd understand,' I said, relieved.

'Understand what?'

'Today was the first time I've seen Marlon since my operation and . . . well, we argued this morning and we've barely said five sentences to each other since.'

'Who's not talking to whom?'

'I guess I'm not talking to him,' I admitted.

'Why?'

'I just told you why.' I frowned. I could feel Nan's sympathy for my point of view evaporating.

'Because he made a mistake?' Nan raised her eyebrows.

'It was a bit more than that,' I protested.

Nan sighed. 'Cameron, in this life you'll find that when you get right down to it, things are rarely as complicated as they seem. It seems to me quite simple really. Your friend made a mistake – something we all do, including you. You now have to decide if you're going to spend the rest of your life bearing a grudge or not. And believe me, life is too short for that kind of nonsense. Even at my advanced years, life is too short.'

I stared at Nan. Was that really what I was doing? 'I don't bear grudges.'

'Glad to hear it,' said Nan. 'Don't start either. So did anything else happen today?'

I looked at Nan and shook my head. Now that the moment had arrived, I didn't want to tell her about Julie. I didn't want to tell anyone. Just thinking about it did funny things to my insides. After my operation I thought I'd be just like everyone else. That was my whole reason for doing it. Only I hadn't realized that some people like Julie and her mum might think otherwise.

I thought about the times before my operation when every time I'd looked up from my desk Julie was there smiling at me. I think Marlon was right. Julie had liked me before my operation. Now all that had changed. It was strange the way things worked out.

'Come on, Cam. Don't get too comfy – we have dinner to make.' Nan leapt to her feet.

I followed more slowly. I had a lot to think about. 'Nan,' I said as she headed out of the door.

'Yes, dear?'

'I'm glad you're here.'

'Of course you are!' Nan smiled. 'And it seems to me I arrived only just in time!'

When we got to the kitchen, Nan started by investigating the fridge. 'I think some of my fried chicken, some baked potatoes and veggies ought to do the trick.'

'Your fried chicken?' I asked suspiciously. 'Does that involve just taking some chicken out of a packet and putting it in the oven or is there chopping and slicing and dicing involved?'

'Taking some chicken out of a packet?' Nan was scandalized. 'I don't think so!'

'Can I watch?' I asked, hoping Nan wouldn't spot what I was trying to do.

'No, you can help!' she replied at once. 'You may be smart, child, but I'm smarter!'

Worth a try!

'The first thing you can do though,' said Nan, 'is change the light bulb in the spare bedroom for me. I want to see where I'm going when I go to bed tonight, before I end up sleeping on the window sill!'

'OK, Nan,' I said, glad to get out of the cooking. Now all I had to do was drag out changing the light bulb for an hour or so, until the worst was over.

'I want you back down here in five minutes – maximum,' said Nan. 'Or I'll come upstairs to fetch you – and you don't want that.'

'Are you reading my mind or something?' I asked, impressed.

Nan laughed. 'Now if I told you that, you'd know as much as I do!'

I went over to the light-bulb drawer. When I opened it, it was like opening a jack-in-the-box. Letters and more letters sprang out of it, falling to the floor. Huffing impatiently I squatted down to pick them up.

'Let me do that,' Nan said quickly.

'It's OK, I've got them.' I waved her off.

'No, Cameron, you go and change the light bulb.'

I frowned up at Nan. She was nervous, agitated. What was her problem? Did she think my new heart might collapse with the strain of squatting down? I smiled to reassure her. 'Nan, I'm here now. It'll only take me two seconds. And Dr Bryce didn't say anything about not bending down!'

As I reached out for a handful of the papers, I caught sight of my name on one of the letters. So I picked it up and read it.

And I wish I hadn't.

L.E.P.A.R.
LEAGUE FOR THE PROTECTION OF ANIMAL RIGHTS

Mr and Mrs Kelsey,

We at LEPAR find you totally immoral and despicable. How could you condone the suffering of innocent animals — because that's what you've done by allowing your son Cameron to have the heart of a pig transplanted into his body. Pigs are intelligent animals with thoughts and feelings just like yourselves. Would you feel it right to have humans bred for the sole purpose of being killed to allow others to use their organs? If it is not right for humans, why do you feel that such action is right and correct for animals?

We understand your concern for your son. Heart disease is

a terrible affliction but it is your attempted solution that we find so reprehensible . . .

I didn't read any more. I couldn't. I picked up another of the letters. It was even worse, rage and anger spilling from every word on the page. I picked up another and another. Threats and more threats made against me, against Mum and Dad, against our house, our car. It was horrible. Some of the letters accused Mum and Dad of only letting me have the operation so they could cash in on the resulting publicity. Some were from animal lovers who sympathized with Mum and Dad's position but asked if they had explored all the options. Some were actually from people wishing us well but they were few and far between. Most were just nasty.

Profoundly shocked, I looked up at Nan. 'Have you seen these?' I asked.

'Some of them,' Nan admitted. 'They're today's batch of letters. I read some of them when I arrived this morning. I didn't know your mum had put them in there. I wish she'd told me.'

'Today's batch?' I stared. 'You mean we get these every day?'

'Every single day.'

'But why do Mum and Dad keep them?' I looked down at the pile of letters again. It couldn't have been more loathsome if it'd been a pile of horse manure on the kitchen floor.

'The police advised them to keep the worst ones — just in case someone tries something. So each night, after you're in bed, they go through them.'

I picked up another.

'No, Cameron. Put it down. Don't read any more,' Nan ordered gently.

'These people hate me. They don't even know me and they hate me. What've I ever done to *them*?' I said, bewildered.

'Cameron, it's not you. It's what you represent. You mustn't take it personally.'

But how could I take it any other way? These people really hated me and Mum and Dad for what we'd done. I shook my head. 'Why didn't Mum and Dad tell me?'

'What for? Why upset you too?'

'Can't the police do something about them?'

'Like what? People are perfectly free to post letters wherever and whenever they please in this country,' said Nan.

'Do people really believe that Mum and Dad only let me have the operation for the money they could make?' I asked, appalled at the very idea of it.

'Some do. Your dad has had to put up with a lot of nonsense at work and your mum reckons her company is on the verge of letting her go. They keep getting inundated with people trying to get in touch with her.'

'But she's not going back until next week.'

'Well, these people either don't know that, or don't believe it, or just don't care,' said Nan.

She bent down to pick up the letters, some still in their envelopes, most just crumpled sheets of paper.

'That's why Mum and Dad wouldn't take the money those two newspapers offered, isn't it?' I realized. 'Because then all those people who accused them of only doing it for the money would think they were right.'

'Your mum and dad wouldn't have taken that money no matter what the circumstances,' Nan told me firmly.

We stuffed the letters back in the drawer. Nan took out a light bulb before firmly pushing the drawer shut. 'Now, I believe you were going to change my light bulb.' She handed the bulb to me.

I nodded and turned to leave the room.

'Cameron?'

'Yes, Nan?'

'Don't let it get you down – OK?'

I forced a smile as I left the kitchen, thinking it was much too late for that. Thousands and thousands of people out there didn't know anything about us except what they'd read in the newspapers and yet, to them, we were the scum of the earth. And Julie and her mum were among them. I told myself not to mind, not to let them get to me but I'd be lying if I said that at that moment, I didn't feel like shouting at the top of my voice or kicking something.

Chapter Twenty-One

Blood

I jiggled about impatiently as Dad asked Dr Bryce about the weather in Yorkshire. When was he going to get to the point?

'No . . . No, Cameron's fine. He wants to go swimming tomorrow so I thought I'd check with you first,' said Dad and, from his tone of voice, it sounded as if he wanted the doctor to say no. 'Yes . . . OK, I'll put him on,' he said reluctantly and handed me the phone.

'Hi, Dr Bryce.'

'Hello, Cameron. How're you feeling?'

'Fine, thanks.'

'I'll be down on Friday to give you your weekly check-up,' said Dr Bryce. 'You're doing so well I think we can make them fortnightly, and we'll see about your local hospital taking over some of your care.'

'Great,' I replied. 'Can I go swimming tomorrow?'

'Well, swimming is very good exercise so I don't see why not, as long as you don't overdo it. Take it easy and don't stay in for longer than half an hour. Don't forget you've got to build up slowly. We don't want to push it.'

'Don't worry. I'll be careful.' I grinned down the phone.

'Could you pass me back to your father, please?' asked the doctor.

I gave the phone back to Dad. 'Dr Bryce says I can go,' I told him and I charged up the stairs. I could make it all the way to the top without pausing or having to stop and catch my breath. I still couldn't get over that.

'Dr Bryce isn't your dad,' Dad called after me, adding apologetically, 'Excuse me, Dr Bryce, I didn't mean to yell in your ear.'

I stuck my head over the banister on the landing. 'So can I go or not?'

'Cam, I'm on the phone.'

'Dad?'

'Just a sec, Dr Bryce.' Dad put his hand over the mouthpiece. 'OK, but I'll come with you.'

'No way!' I was appalled. 'I'm not dragging you around with me everywhere I go like unwanted luggage.'

'Thank you very much!' Dad raised his eyebrows.

'No, I mean it, Dad. You can't come with me. I'd never live it down. All the other boys would think I was a right sissy!'

Dad frowned. 'Oh, all right then. You can go, but only if you promise to—'

'I promise!' I called back and ran into my room.

I was going swimming. And this was only the start. At that moment, I really and truly believed I was going to live for ever. And it felt wonderful.

When at last the buzzer sounded, half the class leapt out of their seats before Mr Stewart could finish his sentence. 'Er . . . complete the next two exercises for your homework and I want it first thing on Thursday morning – and no excuses,' Mr Stewart shouted above the noise.

He legged it out of the room, leaving us to it. I was going swimming immediately after school but at that moment I wasn't thinking about swimming. I only had one thing on my mind – Julie. I marched straight over to her table, where she stood talking to her friends.

Julie,' I said, standing behind her.

When she turned, I deliberately coughed in her face without covering my mouth. That would teach her. She shied away, wiping her face vigorously with her hands.

'I'm just giving you some of my piggy germs,' I told her viciously.

I walked back to my desk, aware that everyone in the class was watching. As I sat down, Marlon turned to look at me but he didn't say a word.

Andrew prodded me in the back. 'Cam, that wasn't very nice.'

'Neither was what she said to me yesterday,' I reminded him.

'And that makes it OK, does it?' Andrew asked.

I glared at him, but as I looked around the class I saw something I'd never seen on the faces of everyone around me - dislike. And as I turned to look at Julie, to my horror I saw that she was crying. It was such a shock. I thought she'd flare up or scream at me or call me all the names under the sun – but she was crying. I bent my head and pretended to be looking for something in my bag. But inside I was choking up, I was so ashamed of myself. I felt like dirt. How could I have done that? All day I'd been thinking of some way to get my own back on Julie and everyone else like her who thought I was untouchable so now that I'd done it, why didn't I feel any better? I retrieved a crumpled but clean tissue from my bag and went over to Julie. Without a word, I held it out to her. She knocked my hand away and turned her back on me.

The tissue fluttered to the ground. I went back to my desk, knowing that I'd blown it.

'You've changed since your operation, d'you know that?' Andrew told me as we walked along.

'No, I haven't.'

'Yes, you have.'

'How?' It was as if every atom in my body had become still, waiting for the answer.

'You're more pushy,' said Andrew.

'I think the word you're looking for is *confident*,' I said.

'And you're more arrogant.' Andrew was getting into his stride now.

'Sure of myself,' I corrected.

'Full of yourself,' Andrew amended.

I looked at Rashid and Marlon. They didn't say a word but it was obvious who they agreed with.

'And where did all this come from?' I asked bitterly.

'Before, you would never have treated Julie like that, no matter what the provocation,' Andrew replied without hesitation. 'That was more like something Travis would do.'

That stung. 'So you think all this is because of my new heart, do you?' I asked scathingly.

'I'm not Julie,' said Andrew. 'A heart is just a pump. It's not the real you, that's all.'

'But you're saying that the real me has become pushy and arrogant — just 'cos I can stand up for myself now?'

'I don't know.' Andrew shrugged. 'Maybe it's just the contrast. Before, you wouldn't say boo to a flea and now it's like you don't take any prisoners.'

We carried on walking in silence. The frown on my face cut deeper and deeper. Any second now and it would be visible on the back of my head. Was that really what my friends thought? Was that really who I was becoming? Rashid and Andrew started chatting about something else and walked on ahead, leaving Marlon and me trailing behind.

I tried to find something to say. I risked a quick

glance at Marlon. He had his hands in his jacket pockets and he was looking very smart.

'Nice jacket.' It came out of my mouth from nowhere.

Faster than I could blink, Marlon's face whooshed bright red! I *knew* I was right. Andrew and Rashid were ahead of us by a couple of metres and I wanted it to stay that way. This was between me and Marlon.

'And the shoes are new too, right?'

'Yes,' Marlon mumbled.

'I suppose your whole family have new clothes now. What else did you all buy? A new car? New furniture? A new house?'

'We haven't got a new house. And Dad only sold your story so that we could keep our old one,' Marlon rounded on me.

I frowned. 'What're you talking about?'

'The bank were about to repossess our house 'cos Mum and Dad couldn't afford the mortgage any more. Since Dad lost his job, things have been really hard for us.'

I glared at Marlon.

'I know that doesn't excuse what Dad did, or make it right,' Marlon continued hastily. 'But that's why he did it – so we wouldn't lose our home.'

'Your mum and dad were meant to be friends with my family.' I couldn't keep the frost out of my voice. 'I bet my dad wouldn't do something like that – no matter how close he was to losing his house.'

197

'Yeah, right!' Marlon began to raise his voice. 'So what would your dad do? Let you all get chucked out on the pavement?'

'He wouldn't have betrayed you to keep his house.'

'Are you sure about that?' Marlon asked. 'Are you telling me that if you were in my dad's shoes, you wouldn't have done exactly the same thing?'

'I . . .' My mouth snapped shut. I thought about Marlon's dad, desperately trying to think of a way to keep his home. Would I really have done any different? Marlon and I walked on in silence. Andrew and Rashid cast the occasional glance back at us. They were probably wondering what all the raised voices were about.

'What would *you* have done?' I asked curiously.

Marlon shrugged. 'To be honest, I don't know. I don't like to think I could've done the same thing, but I don't know.'

'So did your dad pay off the mortgage then?' I asked at last.

'Yeah. The mortgage arrears and all the other debts Mum and Dad had have been paid off. There was just enough money left over for a new pair of shoes for me and Tasha, and a new jacket for me. We're not about to jet off to the Bahamas for a long holiday, believe me.'

I sighed. What was I going to do? Bear a grudge or let it go? 'Well, it's done now.' I shrugged. 'My bleating about it isn't going to change that.'

Silence.

'So how's Tasha?' I asked.

This was ridiculous. Marlon and I were struggling to find things to say to each other. We'd never had to do that before. Usually the two of us could talk about anything and everything and we did. But not today. I wondered if we ever would again.

'Tasha's fine. Her class went to the Science Museum today, I think,' Marlon replied.

We carried on walking in a floundering silence until Rashid and Andrew took pity on us. They took over the conversation then, talking about the last time both of them had visited the Science Museum. Marlon and I lapsed back into silence. I sighed inwardly. It was really scraping the bottom of the barrel when I had to ask Marlon about his younger sister! Marlon and I joined in the conversation but I noticed that we only ever spoke in response to what Andrew or Rashid said. By the time we reached the swimming pool I was desperate for Marlon and me to behave normally with each other again. I tried smiling at him to let him know that everything was OK but although he smiled back, he didn't seem to have much to say.

Things will be better once we're in the pool, I told myself. Marlon, Andrew and the others always had fun in the pool, only this time I'd be having fun with them.

'Who's on for Daredevil Dive?' Andrew laughed.

'I am!' I got in before anyone else could answer.

Suddenly all my friends' eyes were on me.

'Are you sure?' Andrew asked seriously.

'Yep!'

'Don't you think you should wait a bit first?' asked Rashid. 'I mean, you have to dive and touch the bottom of the pool in the deep end. It's a long way down.'

'Don't worry. I can handle it. And if I can't get to the bottom, I'll just come up again, that's all.'

'Cam, I'm not sure this is such a good idea . . .' Andrew began.

'No, if he wants to play Daredevil Dive, let him.'

I wasn't the only one who was surprised by Marlon's words. Usually he was the first one to tell me not to do things, to urge me to be cautious. I wondered at his sudden change of heart.

'Cam hates people to fuss over him,' Marlon said, looking directly at me. 'Besides, he's probably fitter than all of us put together with his new pig's heart.'

Something inside me went very still and alert when he said that. What was he getting at? There was a note in his voice, a peculiar tone that I didn't recognize.

'If you're sure it's safe . . .' Andrew was still doubtful.

'Don't worry about me,' I said. 'Just prepare to get beaten!'

'Big talk from a small peanut head!' Andrew laughed.

'We'll see who's a peanut head!' I told him.

We all lined up at the side of the pool. I could feel my heart begin to beat faster with anticipation. I was exhilarated – this was something I'd never thought I'd be able to do a few months ago. But I must admit, part of me was a bit scared. I hadn't been at the deep end of the pool since before my heart went bad. And Dr Bryce had told me not to push it.

'Ready . . .'

Maybe I shouldn't be doing this.

'Steady . . .'

But it was too late now.

'GO!'

We all swam out to the middle of the pool, then dived. I kicked my legs, telling myself I could do it. Two weeks after my operation I'd been on a running machine at Dr Bryce's clinic with pods stuck all over my chest so that the doctors could monitor my heart when I exercised. Every day I'd had to do that. I'd started off with some gentle walking until, by the end of the six weeks, they had me jogging comfortably. Of course, with the jogging I didn't have to hold my breath as well. I opened my eyes, ignoring how they stung because of the chlorine in the water. I could see that Andrew and Rashid were ahead of me. I had time to wonder where Marlon was before my lungs began to protest and I could hear my heart hammering and my blood roaring. I wasn't going to make it to the bottom. If I carried on much further, I wouldn't be able to make it back up to the surface either. I turned in the water and headed up again. I could see Marlon just behind me. I passed him as I kicked, desperate to try and make it back up to the surface before my lungs exploded. When my head emerged from the water, I gasped in air as if my life depended on it – which at that moment was precisely how it felt. I floated on my back while I dragged breath after breath down into my lungs. When at last I felt my racing heart slow down, I turned and swam slowly back to the side of the pool. I obviously wasn't as fit as I thought I was.

I mean, I didn't expect to win – although it would've been nice! – but I had thought I'd do better. I'd barely made it halfway down. I thought Marlon wouldn't bother going all the way down to the bottom of the pool. I thought he'd come up and gloat – but he didn't. Andrew emerged first, followed by Rashid. Marlon came swimming up last.

'I can't believe it, I beat you.' Andrew grinned at Marlon.

Marlon shrugged. 'Everyone has an off day.'

'And what happened to you?' Rashid asked me.

I smiled. 'I decided it'd be too humiliating for you if I beat you on my very first attempt, so I decided to wait until next week to kick your butt! Same time, same place!'

'You wish!'

'Dream on!'

I looked at Marlon and we both burst out laughing. And as we laughed, the last of the anger and hurt I felt evaporated.

'You think you're bad, don't you!' Marlon teased.

'I don't think it, I *know* it!' I replied.

It was one of the best afternoons of my life. I couldn't do everything my friends did, but I didn't do too badly. And best of all, Marlon and I were talking again. I ended up staying in the water for an hour, which was about forty-five minutes longer than I usually managed. By the time I got out of the water I was as wrinkled and crinkled as a walnut, but I'd never felt better.

I was the first one to get dressed so I bought myself a packet of salt and vinegar crisps from the leisure centre vending machine. I managed to gobble down three-quarters of the packet before the others arrived.

'Who's on for a chicken burger and chips?' asked Rashid.

'You bet!'

'Good idea.'

'Cam, you can have a bacon burger,' Andrew told me.

'Or a couple of pork chops,' Rashid laughed. 'If you don't mind eating your cousins!' Andrew was doubled up with laughter now.

I glared at him, my lips pursed, my face stony. 'Blow it out your ear, Rashid.' I told him.

They all creased up at that. I had to admit my lips did twitch a bit. Eating my cousins! Yeuch! What an idea!

'I'll just go and phone my mum first,' I said, licking my salty fingers. 'She was meant to pick me up and drive

203

me back home. I'll ask her if I can go with you first.'

'Why d'you need your mum to drive you back home?' Andrew asked.

I looked at Marlon, then immediately looked away again. I didn't want him to think I was blaming him – 'cos I wasn't. 'We've been getting one or two weirdo letters, that's all,' I shrugged. 'Some people out there think Trudy shouldn't have died to save my life.'

'Trudy?' asked Rashid.

'That was the name of the pig I got the heart from,' I explained.

'How d'you know that?'

'It's a long story.' I certainly wasn't going to go into that now!

'These weirdo letters, what do they say?' asked Marlon.

'Just that Mum and Dad and I ought to be ashamed and that we're immoral. That sort of thing. Anyway, if you guys wait here, I'll go and phone Mum.' I walked over to the pay phone in the foyer before Marlon could ask me any more questions. I could see him getting more upset with every word I said. I didn't want him to feel guilty about it. It wasn't his fault. I stuck my phone card in the slot and dialled Mum's mobile number. She'd written it down on a piece of paper for me even though I told her not to. I was convinced I'd remember it, but in the end it turned out to be just as well she did. Mum's mobile was on the hall table next to our still unplugged phone. Dad would still be at work, so that was all right, but it was a toss-up between who would answer the phone – Mum or my nan. I hoped it would be Nan – then I could go with my friends for sure. Mum would be harder to get round.

'Hello?'

My heart sank. It was Mum. 'Hello, Mum. Can I go for a burger with Marlon and the others?' I asked.

'Cameron, I don't think that would be a good idea.' Mum's reply was immediate.

'Please, Mum,' I begged. 'I'm fine and besides, no one except my friends knows where I am. Please can I go? Please?'

'And how would you get home?'

'I'll phone you from the precinct as soon as we've finished our burgers. Then you can come and pick me up,' I said eagerly.

'I don't know, Cameron . . .'

'*Please?*'

There was a long pause.

'OK then, but you're to phone me within the next hour without fail,' Mum said sternly. 'D'you understand?'

'Thanks, Mum.'

'The next hour, Cameron. I mean it.'

'Yes, I know.'

'And be careful. Your face has been all over the telly

and the newspapers. Someone might recognize you. On second thoughts—'

''Bye, Mum,' I said and I quickly put down the phone. I'd really get it in the neck for that, but I was having such a good day, I didn't want it to end.

'I can go,' I told my friends.

'Great! What're we waiting for?' said Andrew. 'I'm starving.'

And we all headed for the exit.

'I'm sorry about all those weirdo letters you've been getting,' Marlon said as we walked out of the leisure centre.

'You didn't write them, so it's not your fault,' I said.

'But if I'd kept my mouth shut . . .'

'Let it go, Marlon.' I smiled. 'I have.'

Marlon looked at me and smiled back. I made a fist and playfully tapped him on the jaw. He made a fist and did the same. Then we both grabbed each other and had a wrestle down on the ground.

'Aahhh!' Andrew gave a mock sigh. 'A Kodak moment!'

Marlon and I sprang up at that and told Andrew where to go! We all ended up walking along the road in fits of laughter.

'Are you Cameron Kelsey?'

I turned my head, still beaming away. A woman with light-brown hair, a smart charcoal-grey suit and a smiling face stood behind me. I turned all the way round.

'Are you Cameron Kelsey, the pig-heart boy?' the woman repeated. She had a nice smile, a friendly smile.

Her smile was all I could see as I nodded. Was she a journalist seeking an interview? Maybe she wanted my autograph? The woman brought her hands out from behind her back. Then all time slowed right down. I could see everything, hear everything, because each second seemed to lost so much longer. I was surprised to see she had a bucket in one hand. The woman used her free hand to steady the bucket as she raised it. I saw it had something red in it. Red liquid, sloshing around. Red paint? Some of the liquid spilt over the side of the bucket and hit the pavement, splashing up onto my white trainers. The woman raised the bucket higher. Suddenly aware of what was about to happen, I raised my hands in protest. I opened my mouth to say, NO! And in that moment I was drenched. The red liquid hit me full in the face like a stinging punch. It filled my mouth and stung my eyes and ran down my face like a red river. Only it wasn't paint. I could taste it. It was blood.

'. . . murderer! Murderer! MURDERER!' The woman kept screaming at me, over and over. Over and over and over. I spat, then retched all over my shoes and the pavement. My salt and vinegar crisps mixed with the blood at my feet. Wiping the blood out of my eyes, I stared at the woman.

'MURDERER!'

By this time Marlon was at my side and shouting abuse at the woman. And then, just like that, we were suddenly surrounded. Yet I couldn't take my eyes off the woman before me. She was still screaming at me, ignoring Marlon, and never before had I seen such rage, such hatred on someone's face. Rage and hatred directed at me. Without warning she flew at me, but a man and a woman in the crowd around us pulled her back – which was probably just as well. I couldn't have moved if my life had depended on it.

I don't remember much after that. The police arrived and I was asked a lot of questions that I didn't answer because I couldn't open my mouth. Marlon did a lot of talking for me. Then I was bundled into a car and the next thing I knew I was at the casualty department of my local hospital. And still I couldn't speak. It was as if I was floating outside my body, watching everything that was going on but unable to take part in any of it. I was taken to a cubicle where I was cleaned up and then helped up onto a hospital bed. After the nurse had taken my temperature and blood pressure and checked me over, a cup of hot, sweet tea was forced into my hands. I drank it because one of the nurses told me to – and because I was so cold. My whole body was freezing. Not numb where you can't feel anything, but cold enough to feel as if my body was burning. The tea scalded my lips and burnt my tongue but I drank it anyway. The tea helped a bit, so when they offered me another cup, I nodded immediately. When I looked up from my empty cup, Mum and Nan had arrived. I don't remember much about what happened then either. Nan came and sat down on the chair beside my bed and she held my hand without saying a word. Mum left the cubicle to talk to the doctors and nurses and then to the two policemen who'd brought me to the hospital. I could hear her voice but I couldn't tune in to a single word she was saying.

After I don't know how long I turned to Nan. 'I want to go home now, please,' I said.

Nan stood up and put her arm around me.

'Nan,' I whispered, 'was it worth it?'

She instantly knew what I was talking about. 'Cameron, only you can decide that,' she told me.

'Would you have done it?'

'What? Had the transplant operation?'

I nodded.

'To be honest, I don't know,' Nan replied, 'but I don't think so. I don't think I'm as brave as you.'

Funny but that was just what Travis had said. I remembered how I'd cut him dead and swanned off. Andrew was right. I was no better than Travis. I slid down until I was more lying than sitting and pulled the white cellular blanket up over me. Inside I was still cold. 'I'm not brave, Nan. Stupid maybe, but not brave.'

'Don't say that.' Nan rounded on me at once. 'It

took a great deal of courage to go through with that operation.'

'Desperation, you mean.'

'Cameron, that's enough. That woman earlier was obviously a couple of eggs short of the full breakfast. Are you going to just curl up and give in now? Are you going to let her do that to you?'

Long moments passed as Nan and I looked at each other. Finally I forced a smile. 'I suppose not.'

'Pardon?'

'I guess not.'

'I still can't hear you.'

'NO!' I replied.

We both started laughing at that. Nan had heard my first answer. She just wanted me to say it until I believed it. As my smile faded, I did feel slightly better but I still didn't have the answer to my question. I still didn't know if all this was worth it. I wondered if I ever would.

Chapter Twenty-Two

Holding On

Hello, Alex,

Yes, it's me – your favourite brother. Actually, I'm not in a very jokey mood at the moment. I'm not in a very smiley mood either. A woman, a stranger, threw a bucket of blood over me today. It turns out it was pig's blood. The police are still trying to find out where she got it from but apparently she's not saying a word.

She didn't have much to say to me either when she threw the bucket of blood all over me. She just kept saying one word over and over. Murderer. She called me a murderer. I'm not a murderer. I'm just a boy, doing the best I can. I'm against animal experiments where it isn't necessary and I think using animals to test cosmetics and perfumes and that sort of stuff is obscene, but I read on the Internet that there have been major medical advances that have depended on animal research – like anaesthetics and the diphtheria vaccine and drugs for asthma and drugs for high blood pressure and heart transplants and insulin for diabetics and treatments for leukaemia and . . . and penicillin to treat infections.

Is all that wrong? I don't know any more. I feel I don't know anything any more. I think of that woman and I can't even hate her. Maybe I will later. Maybe I'm still in shock. I don't know what I would've done if my friends hadn't been there — especially Marlon. We were having such a great time. Then it all got spoilt.

Because of her.

Because of me.

We'd all been swimming. I used to be quite good at swimming before I caught the viral infection that started all this. We played Daredevil Dive — that's where you have to dive to the bottom of the deep end and then come back up and race to the side. I didn't make it to the bottom. I ran out of breath. Marlon usually comes first when it comes to Daredevil Dive but today he came last. D'you know, I've only just realized why. I think he stayed back deliberately to keep an eye on me. I wonder why I didn't realize that at the time.

So, here I am — clean again. I swallowed some of the blood that woman threw at me. My mouth, was open and it went in my mouth and ran down my throat. I was as sick as a . . . a pig . . . afterwards, but how do I know all that stuff is out of my stomach? The doctors tried to reassure me that I only swallowed a minute quantity and because I was sick immediately afterwards it's very unlikely that any was left in my system — but how can they know for sure? I had a shower when I got home. A shower that lasted for an hour and a half. I let the water run into my mouth and down my throat. I don't think I should've done that. Shower water isn't the same as tap water, but I couldn't help it. I can still taste that foul stuff in my mouth. I've used up a brand-new tube of toothpaste brushing my teeth for half an hour. I'm all clean again, so why do I still feel so dirty? Why do I still feel as if I'm only holding on by my fingertips?

I asked Dad what had happened to the woman who threw the blood. He told me she's been arrested. I can't help wondering where she got the blood from. Dad doesn't know. She wouldn't have killed some poor animal just to throw its blood over me, would she? Anyway, Dad was all for going to the police station first thing in the morning to press assault charges. I must admit, I thought she'd have to have hit me with her bucket to be charged with something like that, but Dad says it is still assault. You should've seen Mum and Dad's face when I asked them not to press charges against the woman. Even now I don't know why I did that. Part of it is that I don't want any more fuss. I don't want a big, drawn-out case with my face in the paper every two seconds. But it was more than that. I want to prove to everyone — and myself, I think — that I'm better than that. Not in a superior, stick-my-nose-in-the-air kind of way, but I've forgiven her, so what's the point of prosecuting her. And I really have forgiven her - which, I must admit, I find astounding! But Nan was right — life is too short to bear grudges. You remember that!

But, Alex, I don't know what to do or where to go from here. All I do know is that I have to get fit and stay fit. I must. I have to show that woman, and Mum and Dad and the whole wide world that all this is for a reason, a good cause.

213

Otherwise, it was all for nothing and what's the point?

You see, Alex, for the first time I'm beginning to wonder if I made a mistake in going through with all this. D'you think I made a mistake? I don't know any more. I don't know anything any more. I just want to . . .

It's all right, I'm not going to cry.

I'm not going to cry . . .

I'm not going to cry . . .

Chapter Twenty-Three

A Favour

'Marlon, could you do me a favour?'

'What's that?'

Five weeks had passed since the bucket of blood incident and unfortunately, for a while, it had stirred up a whole lot of interest in me again. Now Mum insisted on driving me to and from school every day. And going to the leisure centre was out of the question. Mum and Dad wouldn't hear of it. I could still see Mum and Dad's faces when we got home that night. Mum ranted and raved and raged for a good hour, while Dad stood by the front window watching the crowds outside our house and silently seething. Only Nan recognized how I felt. She understood why I wanted to go back to the leisure centre. She understood why I wanted to get things back to normal as soon as possible. But Mum and Dad wouldn't hear of it. And now that Nan had gone back to her own home, I had no one on my side. So the way I saw it, Mum and Dad left me no choice.

Thankfully, the second pig-heart transplant had taken

place at Dr Bryce's clinic so I was no longer the sole focus of attention. It made what I was doing easier. It was simple really. I had some problems of my own to sort out.

'Marlon, could you cover for me again tonight?'

'You're not going swimming again, are you?' Marlon asked, upset.

I could tell he wasn't happy with me for the position I was placing him in. Every day for the last week I'd phoned my mum to tell her I was going to his house after school. Then, after my swim, I'd go to his house for ten minutes or so, then phone for Mum or Dad to come and pick me up. I knew that sooner or later I'd be found out, but with a little luck it would be later.

I'd suddenly become obsessed with swimming. Well, not so much with swimming as with Daredevil Diving. I still hadn't made it to the bottom of the pool, but I was going to. I was determined. I had no idea why it was so important to me, but it was. It was as if, by touching the bottom of the pool, I'd be proving something to myself and the rest of the world. Only I had no idea what.

'Cam, you can't keep doing this. You can't go to the leisure centre every evening.'

'Watch me,' I said.

'But suppose someone sees you?' Marlon said unhappily.

'So what? Besides, things are back to normal now. The crowds have gone from outside our house. Our

216

phone's been plugged back in. Nan's gone home. Why should everything else be allowed to return to normal except my life?' I argued.

'Going swimming after school every day isn't normal unless you're training for the Olympics,' said Marlon. 'And you won't even let me come with you.'

'You've got to stay at your house just in case my mum or dad phone,' I said.

'Sooner or later they're going to twig. Grown-ups are stupid but they're not stupid all the time.'

'I know. But I'll have finished by the time Mum and Dad catch me.'

'Finished what?'

I didn't answer. 'So will you cover for me?'

'You know I will.' Marlon replied.

'Of course I know you will.' I smiled at Marlon. ''Cos I know I can trust you.'

Marlon smiled at that but the frown didn't take long to return to his face.

'Marlon and Cameron, would you like to stand up and share your conversation with the rest of the class?' asked Mr Stewart. 'I'm sure we'd all be fascinated to hear what's so riveting that you have to speak while I'm trying to teach.'

I said the first thing that came into my head. 'I was asking Marlon if he'd written a poem for his English homework.'

'And had he?'

'No, sir.'

'And have you?'

'Yes, sir.'

'Let's hear it then,' said Mr Stewart.

I stared at him. 'Er . . . it's not really finished yet.'

'Doesn't matter. Let's hear it.'

'It's not very good.'

'Let's hear it.'

'Sir, it's dire!' I admitted.

The rest of the class tittered at that.

'I'm even more intrigued now. Get it out,' said Mr Stewart. I scowled at him but he wasn't going to change his mind. Reluctantly I dug into my desk. I couldn't believe he was really going to make me read it out. I always knew he was a sadist and here was my proof.

'Sorry, sir. I must've left it at home,' I lied. No way was I going to read out my first attempt at my homework. It was a poem about a butterfly, for goodness' sake. No way was I going to read out anything so weedy.

'That's a shame. I'll have to make sure I ask your English teacher to show me this amazing poem worthy of all that discussion just now,' said Mr Stewart.

'Sorry, sir,' I mumbled.

Mr Stewart got on with the rest of the lesson. Me? I couldn't wait for the lesson to finish. I was desperate to leave and go swimming. Under the water nothing and no one could touch me. Nothing could trouble me. Thank goodness this was the last lesson of the day. As soon as the buzzer went I would make sure I was the first one out of the classroom. In fact the others wouldn't be able to see me for dust. One of the advantages of having a new heart – even if it was from a pig: it made me healthy enough to get out of the class in a hurry.

Take a deep breath, I told myself. And another. And another. Now go!

I struck out for the middle of the pool, kicked back with my legs and dived. Kick, kick, kick. Down, down, down. The water stung my eyes and the further down I went, the more it felt as if giant hands were wrapped around my chest and squeezing. But I kept going. I could see the bottom. Just a little further. But from the pounding of my heart and the raging of the blood in my head, I knew I'd have to turn back now or I wouldn't be able to turn back at all. Cursing my weak body, I headed back up towards the surface of the water, desperately disappointed. Would I ever make it to the bottom? I was beginning to wonder. But I had a more immediate problem – the surface of the swimming pool looked as if it was miles away. I kicked harder, forcing myself to go faster. I broke through the surface of the water just as I thought my lungs must surely burst. I tried to float on my back, but my body was having spasms from trying to drink down air into my starved lungs. I swallowed some water and started coughing and spluttering as I tried to clear my mouth. I twisted round, forcing myself to float, forcing my body to calm down. My heart, which had been racing so fast it seemed to consist of just one continuous beat, began to slow down. But I had a pain in my left shoulder and the left side of my neck. I felt sick and my lungs were hurting and the pain didn't ease as I began to breathe more normally. I made my way to the side of the pool and hauled myself out. Even that was a major effort. I was so tired. I went back to the changing rooms, had a shower and decided to head straight home.

By the time I put my front-door key in the lock the pain in my shoulder had passed, but I still felt a bit sick. I'd been feeling vaguely nauseous for a few days now and it was getting worse, not better. As I closed the front door behind me, I could hear one of Mum's favourite Lenny Kravitz songs playing softly from the living room. I tiptoed to the living-room door, which was open. I peeped through the crack between the door and the door-frame. Mum was sitting on the sofa with her feet up on Dad's lap and Dad was massaging her toes —again!

'That's very relaxing.' Mum smiled at Dad. 'Alex has stopped kicking me and gone to sleep.' She patted her bulging stomach.

'I can't believe I'm massaging your smelly toes again. You are such a smooth talker!' said Dad in his lovey-dovey voice. 'You could talk the man in the moon into giving you a green cheese sandwich!'

'I don't want the man in the moon. I just want you.' Mum smiled, making me want to throw up!

'What is it with you two and toes?' I asked, going into the room.

Mum frowned. 'What're you doing here? I thought you were at Marlon's?'

'I was. I decided to come home by myself.'

Mum swung her feet off Dad's lap. 'You came home by yourself?' Her voice was sharp.

'Yes, I did – and nothing happened,' I replied.

'Cameron . . .' I could tell Mum was winding up for a mega-rant.

'Cathy, you can't spend the rest of your life hovering over Cam like a hawk,' Dad said gently. 'Sooner or later he's got to start doing things for himself again. You can't do everything for him.'

'I'm not trying to. I just . . .'

Dad smiled and with that smile Mum's voice trailed off.

'Are you OK?' she asked me at last.

'I'm fine,' I lied. My nausea hadn't passed but I wasn't about to give Mum an excuse to smother me again. I wished Nan was here. I badly wanted to talk to her. 'Mum . . .' I began.

The doorbell rang.

'I'll get it,' I said.

'No,' Mum said at once, 'I'll—'

'Cathy . . .' Dad admonished gently. 'The crowds

have gone, the police have gone and most of the letters have stopped. We can't spend the rest of our time in this house hiding and living in fear.'

I saw Mum take a deep breath. 'I thought you were going to open the door,' she snapped.

I smiled. I knew the snap wasn't directed at me. Even if I lived to be ninety, Mum would still be fussing over me. I went back out into the hall, thinking how nice it was to walk into the house and not hear a major argument going on between Mum and Dad. Things seemed to be working out after all. I opened the front door.

'Dr Bryce!' I said, surprised. 'We only saw you a week ago. You're not due again until after Christmas.'

'I need to see you and your parents,' Dr Bryce told me, with no trace of a smile.

One look at his face and I could see it was serious. Without a word, I stepped aside. Dr Bryce came into the house and headed straight for the living room. I closed the door slowly behind him. I stood out in the hall for a few moments. I didn't want to go into the living room. I was afraid of what I would hear. Maybe if I stayed out in the hall, then whatever it was wouldn't be about me and wouldn't affect me. But it didn't work that way. Whatever it was, it wouldn't go away just because I wanted to do my ostrich act and bury my head in the hall carpet. I walked into the living room.

Mum and Dad were sitting on the sofa with Mum's

feet now firmly on the ground. Dr Bryce was in the armchair. They all watched me as I sat down next to Dad.

'I've got some bad news.' Dr Bryce didn't even attempt to beat about the bush. He turned and looked directly at me. 'To put it simply, Cameron, your white blood cell count is way up.'

'My T-cells or my B-cells?' I asked.

Dr Bryce was too worried to be impressed. 'How much do you know about the way your immune system and your white blood cells work?'

'Only what we've done in biology and what I've read in books and over the Internet,' I admitted.

'Hang on. What does all this mean exactly?' Dad asked quietly.

A deep silence filled the room. 'It means-' Dr Bryce began.

'It means that maybe my body is starting to reject my new heart,' I interrupted, never taking my eyes off the doctor.

'Not necessarily. It may just mean that we need to rethink the dosage and content of your anti-rejection and immuno-suppressant drugs. The trouble with all these drugs is that it's a fine balancing act between what and how much of each drug you should get.'

'I thought you said you'd developed a new drug, a complement blocker that would stop Cameron's body rejecting his heart.' Mum's expression was stony.

'We have. I think, I *hope* we just need to amend the dosage. Cameron, I've brought you a new series of injections which I'd like you to start taking immediately. I'll take the old ones back with me.'

'More injections.' Mum said, dismayed.

'We've reached a deal with a pharmaceutical company only this week. They've agreed to start manufacturing the drug in tablet form from the New Year. We don't have the resources at my clinic to do that, so hopefully the injections won't be for too much longer. Cameron, I also want to change the immunosuppressant tablets you're taking. I think we need to be more aggressive.'

'Will all this work?' I asked.

'It's impossible to tell. All we can do at this stage is monitor you closely, and keep fine-tuning the dosages of the various drugs you need to stop your body rejecting your new heart.'

Dr Bryce dug into his large briefcase and brought out a clear plastic box full of vials. 'We don't want your body to reject your new heart but at the same time we don't want to leave your immune system so weak that you couldn't fight off a cold if you caught one.'

'I understand.' I nodded.

'How have you been feeling, Cameron? Have you been feeling more tired than normal? Or maybe a bit ill?'

'No.' I shook my head. 'I've been feeling fine. Great in fact.'

224

'Hhmm!' Dr Bryce studied me. 'I think I should go back to seeing you weekly rather than monthly.'

'But what about my fortnightly check-ups at the local hospital? D'you still want me to go there as well?'

'Yes, I think so. I'll speak to the hospital. I also want to change a few of the tests you regularly have.'

I shrugged. 'OK. If you think I should.'

'I do,' Dr Bryce replied.

'Well, I'd better go upstairs and get on with my homework,' I said, jumping to my feet.

No one told me to stay, so I didn't. I left the room and forced myself to run up the stairs, even though I was dog-tired. When I got to my room, I chucked myself down on my bed, gasping for breath. My heart was pounding again. I told myself that the stairs weren't responsible for my racing pulse, it was Dr Bryce's news – but I knew that was only partly true.

I thought of Alex downstairs waiting to be born, but the thought hurt. So I turned my thoughts to the swimming pool at my local leisure centre instead.

'I'll make you a deal,' I spoke to my new heart. 'I'll play Daredevil Dive just one more time. If I manage to touch the bottom of the pool then you have to stay inside me and not cause any more trouble. And you . . .' I spoke to the rest of my body. 'And you have to leave my heart alone and let it get on with pumping my blood around my body. OK, everyone? I'll try to touch the bottom of the pool just one more time. And if I manage it, then we all live together until we're ninety. Agreed?'

It was agreed.

I'd go to the pool after school tomorrow. I was in control once again. Not my body, not my heart – but me. All I had to do was touch the bottom of the pool. My future was now back in my own hands.

Chapter Twenty-Four

Losing

'Marlon, I still don't know why you're here,' I said crossly.

Today of all days, I didn't want any company while I swam. Today was too important. I was scared but determined. Touching the bottom of the pool was like tossing a coin. Heads I win. Tails I lose.

'I like to swim occasionally too,' Marlon replied.

'But it's not even Tuesday. You and the others only ever come swimming on a Tuesday.'

Marlon smiled at me. 'There's no law that says I can't come swimming on a Thursday instead.'

I was about to argue but I thought better of it. If I protested too much, Marlon might realize that I was up to something. But I was still annoyed. I bundled my bag and my clothes into a locker and banged it shut.

'So what've you been doing here every afternoon, anyway?' asked Marlon as we both made for the pool.

'Just kicking about and swimming. I've been trying to build up my strength and stamina. Swimming is brilliant exercise,' I replied, in what I hoped was an off-hand manner.

'Fancy a race? Just a width but underwater?' Marlon challenged.

Under normal circumstances I would've snatched his hand off, but these were hardly normal circumstances. I didn't want to waste any of my energy on a race. I knew I didn't have that much energy to spare.

I smiled. 'Maybe later.'

I sat down at the edge of the pool and slipped into the water. It was cool, verging on cold, and made me gasp. I held onto the bar which ran around the side of the pool and kicked out leisurely with my legs to warm myself up a little. Marlon dived straight in and immediately struck out for the other edge of the pool. I watched him for a few moments. I was so glad Nan had talked some sense into me. It was a pain that Marlon had insisted on coming to the pool with me today, but I was glad we were still friends. I think if it hadn't been for Nan I might never have had sense enough to let go of my anger. It was strange the way things turned out. Before my heart operation, everything had seemed so clear. I didn't have long to live so I knew what my priorities were – my family and my friends. Yet after my operation, for a while my priorities had become completely messed up.

So what was important to me now?

I couldn't see past touching the bottom of the pool.

My friends had all done it, but that wasn't the reason. It was a challenge I'd issued to myself. It was my way of proving that I was as good, as healthy, as deserving of life as anyone else. I looked across the pool. Marlon had almost reached the other side. I'd have to act fast.

This was it! Now or never. Do it now, while I was still fresh and had the energy. I let go of the bar and began to tread water.

One . . . two . . . three . . . go! I swam to the middle of the pool, took several deep breaths and dived down and down and down. I didn't stop, even when my lungs screamed at me for air, even when my heart shrieked at me to turn back, even when my blood roared at me to stop. I kicked my legs and went down further.

And I touched the bottom.

It was icy cold beneath my fingers but I had reached it. Elated, I turned round and kicked against the bottom of the pool to give myself an extra push back to the surface. Except the surface was a long way away. And halfway up through the water, I knew I wasn't going to make it.

Consequences

Chapter Twenty-Five

Walking on the Moon

When I opened my eyes, I was lying flat and a brilliant white light was blinding me. I thought I was dead, I really did, until I heard a scraping sound beside me and then Dad's anguished face swam into focus above my own.

I smiled at him but he didn't seem to see it. He stared at me, misery clouding his eyes. I tried to speak, to tell him I was glad to see him, but my mouth didn't seem to want to work.

I'm all right, Dad. I hoped my eyes told him what my mouth could not.

In fact I was better than all right, I was *alive*. The rest could wait. I closed my eyes and fell asleep.

When I woke up, Mum, Dad, Nan, Dr Ehrlich and Dr Bryce were all standing around my bed.

'What happened?' I whispered, confused. Then I remembered the swimming pool. 'How did I get out of the pool?'

'Marlon saved your life,' Mum told me, her expression grim.

'Oh . . . First Dr Bryce, then Marlon.' I tried to laugh, but my throat was still hurting.

'It's not funny, Cameron,' said Dad. 'When you get out of here, you and I are going to have a long talk.'

And at that, Mum burst into tears.

'Mum, don't cry. Please don't cry.' I tried to sit up but I didn't have one gram of strength in my body. 'Mum, you'll upset Alex,' I pleaded. 'Please don't cry. I'm OK now. Really I am.'

'Cameron . . .' Dr Bryce began. He and Dad looked at each other across my bed and I knew in that instant what was coming. 'Cameron, your body is rejecting your new heart.'

'Is that why I've been feeling tired and sick?'

'How long have you felt like that?' Dr Bryce asked me sharply.

'Just a week or so.'

'Why on earth didn't you say? Why didn't you tell me the truth yesterday? We could've taken you into hospital. We could've amended your anti-rejection drug therapy earlier,' Dr Bryce said, distraught.

That was exacdy why I hadn't said anything. I needed to finish what I'd started.

'It's not his fault, it's yours.' Mum rounded on Dr Bryce. 'Why did it take you a week to get the results of his last blood tests?'

'The first set of results got contaminated,' Dr Bryce answered. 'We had to run all the tests again.'

'Mum, it's OK.' I smiled. 'It wouldn't have made any difference.'

'You don't know that,' said Dad.

And yes, he was right. I didn't know that – not for sure, but I felt I was right. 'So what happens now?' I whispered. 'D'you give me more anti-rejection drugs?'

'I don't think we can do that. It would just postpone the inevitable. Your heart is fighting a losing battle. The only way forward now is to have another heart transplant,' he said. 'And we have to act within the next few days before you become too weak to survive the surgery.'

'Another pig-heart transplant?' I asked.

'Yes, of course.'

'Is that the only way?' asked Dad.

'I'm afraid so. I don't think Cameron's heart will last much into the New Year otherwise,' said Dr Bryce.

I smiled at him. I liked the way he was as blunt as ever. The poor man didn't look any happier than my mum and dad. I realized that his brusque manner was his way of coping with things. He must've been through a lot with all the abuse he'd received over the years, with all the abuse he was probably still receiving. 'How's the other heart-transplant patient doing?' I asked.

'She's doing fine. It took her longer to recover than you but now she's making excellent progress,' Dr Bryce replied.

'Good. I'm glad.' And I was. 'I'd hate for all your research to have to stop now.'

Dr Bryce turned to my mum and dad. 'I've spoken to the senior registrar here and she reckons Cameron can probably go home tomorrow – Saturday or Sunday at the very latest. I think if we arrange for Cameron to come back up to the clinic on Tuesday, we'll schedule the surgery for Wednesday and—'

'Dr Bryce, I don't want another transplant operation.'

Dr Bryce wasn't the only one who was shocked by my words. He frowned deeply. 'What're you talking about?'

'I don't want another operation.'

'Why not?'

'Cameron, what're you saying?'

'Cameron, you can't give up now . . .'

'Cameron, have you thought about this . . . ?'

The only one who didn't jump down my throat was Nan.

'Mum, Dad, I don't want another transplant,' I said. 'It's hard to explain but . . .'

'Try,' Mum said immediately.

It really was strange the way things worked out. Mum had been so against the operation at the beginning and now she was the one really pushing me to have another one. 'Would it make a difference if your second transplant was from a human donor rather than a pig?' Dr Ehrlich asked me.

'No,' I replied at once. 'No difference at all.'

'Then why not?' asked Mum.

'Dr Bryce, if I had the second operation, how long would I have to take all those drugs you've been giving me?'

'Probably for the rest of your life – but isn't it worth it if they keep you alive?'

'But they're making me sick and I'm beginning to get tired all the time,' I said quietly. 'It's like before my operation.'

'But as I said, we can fine-tune the dosage until we hit upon a drug regimen that suits you,' Dr Bryce argued.

'But I don't want the rest of my life to be made up of pills and powders and injections and nothing else. I don't want to feel sick and tired all the time.'

'That won't necessarily happen,' said Dr Ehrlich.

'But the second transplant has less chance of succeeding than the first.'

Dad frowned. 'Where did you hear that?'

'I read it on the Internet,' I said.

'You can't believe everything you read,' Dad told me. 'You know that.'

'Yes, I know that. But a while ago, Mum said something about me being special. She told me that I'm not just special because of my heart and I shouldn't think that. But I began to. I began to think that my new heart was all I was. That's why I wanted to touch the bottom of the swimming pool, to prove to myself that I was something more.'

Dr Bryce shook his head. 'I don't understand.'

'I'm not sure I understand myself,' I admitted. 'All I know is, it's the quality of your life that counts, not the quantity. I've been very lucky so far and thank you for everything you did for me, Dr Bryce. I really do appreciate it. But enough is enough. I want my life back. Even if it's only for another few months.'

'And what about Alex?' Mum asked.

'I'm going to try to hang on long enough to see her or him. After that, whatever happens, happens.'

'So you're going to give up?' Dr Ehrlich said.

'Of course he isn't. He just wants to fight in his own way,' said Nan.

I knew Nan would understand.

'But . . .'

'I'm not going to stop taking the anti-rejection treatments,' I said.

'They'll just slow down the process, they won't stop it,' Dr Bryce protested vehemently. 'Cameron, your body will still reject your heart. All you'll do is buy yourself a few more months.'

'That's all I want.' I smiled. 'I want to be able to say goodbye to Alex in person.'

'I don't think you've thought this through . . .' Dr Bryce began.

I tuned him out of my head. I looked up at Nan. She smiled at me and took my hand.

'I want to speak to Cameron alone. Could you all disappear for a while?' she said.

Reluctantly Mum, Dad and the others left my bedside.

'You do understand, don't you, Nan?' I asked anxiously. I hadn't been wrong about that, had I?

'Oh yes.' Nan sat down on the side of my bed. 'You set yourself a goal and now you've achieved it. You've touched the bottom of the swimming pool.'

Something in her voice kept me silent.

'It's a shame you never knew your grandfather. You were named after him, you know.'

I nodded. 'Yes, I know.'

'He died of lung cancer.'

I knew that too. What was Nan driving at?

'He wanted to live so much. He tried everything. He finally gave up his precious cigarettes – although he left that too late. He had chemotherapy, drugs, you name it, he tried it. He wasn't going to give up.'

'And you think that's what I'm doing?'

'Well, you've touched the bottom of the swimming pool.' Nan smiled. 'What else have you got to live for? What else is there worth fighting for?'

I frowned at her. 'That's not how it is.'

'I know,' Nan said gently. 'You feel sick and we both

239

know you'll probably get sicker. You're in pain and it'll probably get worse.'

'Is this meant to make me change my mind?' I raised my eyebrows.

'It's meant to make you think. Cameron, life is very, very precious. Don't let go of it. I watched my Granddad fight and lose – but at least he fought. He fought every step of the way. Can you say the same?'

I turned my head away from her, disappointed. Nan's gentle fingers turned my head to face her again. 'Cameron, you've touched the bottom of the pool – and good for you. If that's what keeps you going, find another challenge. And another one after that. And another one after that. I'm not going to lose you too. Besides, the world needs more Camerons!'

I looked at Nan. My eyes were hurting. 'I'm so tired,' I whispered.

'I know.'

'And I'm scared,' I admitted.

'I know that too. But Cameron, dear, you're allowed to be scared. You're just not allowed to give up – not without a good fight. So put your fists up and come out slugging.'

Silence.

'I can't.' I turned my head away again.

'Cameron . . .'

'No, Nan. I've tried and tried and I can't.' I faced her and it was one of the hardest things I'd ever had to do.

'I don't want to drag this out any longer than necessary. Please don't ask me to. Once I've seen Alex, I'll be happy.'

Nan leaned back in her chair. She didn't smile. She didn't frown. Her face was a mask as she studied me, but I knew she was disappointed. She sighed and stood up. 'Cameron, I could talk to you until I'm blue, green and purple in the face but it wouldn't make any difference,' she said. 'I would give my life if it meant you'd be well again but it doesn't work that way. You have to want it. *You* have to fight. No one can do it for you – not even me.'

'Just now, you said to the doctors that I was fighting in my own way,' I reminded her.

'Lying on your bed feeling sorry for yourself and getting ready to give up is one way of fighting – the easiest, the least productive, saddest way,' Nan told me.

'It's accepting things as they really are, that's all.'

'Rubbish!' Nan retorted. 'But you'll change your mind. I believe in your strength and your common sense. But as I said before, the final decision has to be yours. Just don't let me down or I'll have to give you a good swift kick – and I can do it too! Now let me go and get your mum and dad. You have to decide what you're going to tell them.'

I wiped my eyes with the back of my hand as I watched Nan leave. Touching the bottom of the pool. It seemed so silly now. It was hardly in the same league as walking on the moon or discovering penicillin or something like that. But it had meant so much to me.

Why?

I mean, some people wanted to be millionaires when they grew up and they spent their whole lives trying to achieve that goal. Some people wanted children, some wanted to be doctors or lawyers or to drive a fire engine. Maybe, deep down – so deep down that even I wasn't consciously aware of it – I had never expected this operation to work. Was that it? Or maybe I'd begun to suspect that something was going wrong in the last couple of weeks.

Is that why I came up with something just outside my grasp? Something to work for, something difficult to achieve, but not impossible? Touching the bottom of the pool was my version of walking on the moon.

So what next? Nan was right. Only I could decide that one.

Chapter Twenty-Six

Creeping

When I entered my bedroom, Nan was busy arranging some fresh orange carnations in a vase on my work table.

'Hi, Nan,' I said, eyeing the flowers with suspicion. 'Why're you putting flowers in my room?'

Nan smiled. 'Just to brighten up the place.'

I hadn't seen her for two days – not since our talk at the hospital – and I'd really missed her. But as I looked at her, I couldn't help feeling worried – because she looked frail and very tired. 'Are you all right, Nan?' I asked.

'Of course.' She grinned at me – and suddenly she didn't look fragile at all.

Just looking at her, I knew she was OK. Nan's whole personality shone from her eyes. She was a whirlwind that nothing and nobody could stop.

'And what about you?' asked Nan. 'Have you changed your mind about the operation yet?'

'No, and I'm not going to either,' I said.

Nan sniffed. 'If you say so.'

'You're not going to start lecturing me, are you?' I asked anxiously.

Mum and Dad had gone on about nothing else since I'd let them know of my decision, until I was sick up to the eyebrows of hearing about it. I didn't want the operation and as far as I was concerned, that was that.

'I wouldn't dream of wasting my breath,' Nan told me loftily. 'Besides, you'll change your mind.'

'What d'you mean?'

'I mean, you'll see sense and change your mind. Just don't wait too long.'

'I am not going to change my mind.' I admit I was peeved. 'What makes you think that?'

'Now if I told you that, you'd know as much as I do.' Nan winked at me. And it was such a sly wink, I couldn't help laughing.

'Cam, is there anything I can get you? How about some chicken and a nice salad?'

'No thanks, Nan. I'm not hungry,' I said. 'Besides, I think Mum's downstairs cooking dinner for all of us already.'

'In that case, I think I'll go for a lie down before dinner and catch forty winks – although at my age I need more like eighty!'

Nan removed some imaginary dust from my bedside table and headed for the bedroom door. She stopped before she got there though and gave me a very strange look. 'Cam, you do know you're my favourite grandson, don't you?' she told me.

'So far, I'm your only grandson,' I pointed out.

'True.' Nan chuckled. 'But you do know I love you?'

'Yes,' I said uncomfortably. 'And why are we getting mushy all of a sudden?'

'A little mush now and then never hurt anyone,' she told me. 'Now let me give you a kiss.'

'Do I have to?'

'Yes.'

Reluctantly, I bent my head so that Nan could kiss my cheek. Then she rubbed her fingers over my skin as if she was sanding a rough piece of wood.

'Are you shaving yet?' she asked.

'Nan!'

'Only teasing, Cam. Your skin is as smooth as a baby's bottom – but not as wrinkle-free!'

'Nan, I thought you were going for a lie down.'

'I can take a hint!' Nan smiled. 'See you later, darling.'

''Bye, Nan.' I held the bedroom door open for her.

'Trying to tell me something?'

'No. Just go,' I said.

Nan and I smiled at each other before she headed for the spare bedroom. As I closed my door, I wondered for the first time what Nan did at her home in Bolton. Was she lonely? Did she have many friends? What did she do all day? Nan was never one to sit still, that was for sure. I'd have to ask her when she woke up.

I could hear her now: 'Why the sudden interest? You never asked before.'

'I'm asking now.'

'And I'll think about whether or not I'm going to tell you!'

Just playing the imaginary conversation in my head made me smile. I could talk and argue with Nan in a way that I couldn't with my parents. Not that Nan stood for any nonsense – she wouldn't go for that at all. But she didn't talk down to me and she didn't talk to me like a parent.

'Cameron, could you come downstairs and help with the dinner, please?' Mum yelled.

I sighed. Help with the dinner, my left foot! She and Dad just wanted another chance to try and persuade me to change my mind. Slowly I made my way downstairs. I paused at the kitchen door, took a deep breath and walked in.

An hour later Mum said, 'I think we're about ready to eat now.'

I eyed Mum and Dad with suspicion. What was going on? They hadn't said a single word about Dr Bryce or the operation or anything even remotely medical. I'd just spent the last half an hour washing every salad ingredient we had in the salad crisper and chopping, slicing and dicing. Tonight, for the first time, making the salad was totally down to me. Mum raised an eyebrow, but she didn't say a word when I dropped lumps of chunky peanut butter into the salad. I caught Dad miming sticking his fingers down his throat though, when he thought I wasn't looking.

'Have you put out all the cutlery on the table?' Dad asked.

I nodded.

'Fine.' Mum smiled. 'You can go and get your nan now. If she's still asleep wake her up *gently*.'

What did she think I'd do? Burst into Nan's bedroom with a marching band? I ran up the stairs but only made it three-quarters of the way up before I was out of puff and feeling a bit sick and my heart was sledge-hammering inside my body. I'd almost forgotten what that was like – getting out of puff just going up the stairs. I'd become so used to not just running up them but taking them two and three at a time with energy to spare. Once I began to get my breath back, I walked up the few remaining stairs, a deep frown cutting into my face. Was I really prepared to give it all up – the healthy, lively feeling it had taken me so little time to get used to? A crowd of images burned through my mind – images of me jumping and running and playing football. They were all worth holding onto – weren't they? Yes, there was a downside - pills and medicines and doctors and hospitals and Julie and animal rights extremists. But the upside was *life*. A life worth something. A life worth living. And surely a life worth living was a life worth fighting for. I stopped on the landing, totally confused. I had no idea what I wanted to do. I wanted the operation and yet I didn't. I wanted to fight on and yet I was so tired. What was the matter with me? I wasn't usually so dithery. Was Nan right? Was I changing my mind?

'Nan?' I called softly into the darkened room as I opened the door. 'Nan, dinner's ready.'

I peeped into the room, which was dark except for the low-wattage light coming from the bedside lamp. Nan lay on her side on top of the duvet and facing the door. Her eyes were closed. She was fast asleep. I tiptoed into the room, careful not to make any sudden noises and frighten the life out of her. Up close, she looked so peaceful. She actually had a slight smile on her face. She was obviously having a good dream!

'Nan?' I placed my hand on her upper arm and nudged her gently. 'Dinner's ready. And I made an extra special salad to go with it!' I could just see Nan's face when she found out exactly what my special ingredient was.

'Nan!' I nudged her a bit harder. Her arm, which was resting on her side, slipped backwards off her body and her hand flopped into the duvet, palm up. I stared at her.

'Nan?' I shook her a bit harder. Her whole body tipped over so that she was lying on her back, her eyes still closed. A feeling raced through me – as if every drop of blood in my body had turned to Arctic water. I stepped back, unable to take my eyes off my nan, not even able to blink. Do something. I had to do *something*.

'MUM! DAD!' A scream ripped from me. And once I'd started I couldn't stop.

Dad came bounding up the stairs, closely followed by Mum.

'What is it? What's the matter?' Dad asked anxiously.

I pointed at Nan. Mum took one look at her before rushing over. Dad ushered me out of the room. My feet barely touched the carpet in my haste to get out of there. Because I was frightened. More frightened than I'd ever been before in my life. Even more frightened than I was before my heart transplant operation. As soon as I was on the landing, Dad went back into the spare bedroom, shutting the door behind him. I put my hands against the closed door, praying desperately that I was wrong. That Nan was just asleep.

Please let her be all right. Please. *Please* . . .

My hands fell to my sides as I waited for something, anything to happen. What was going on in there? What were Mum and Dad doing? I turned and walked towards my room, but I didn't make it. Halfway there, I leaned against the wall, before sliding down it. My face was soaking wet with silent tears, and all at once I couldn't keep silent any more. I howled like some kind of wounded animal and curled up in a ball on the floor, where I cried and cried and cried.

I didn't even know Dad had left Nan's room until he sat on the carpet next to me and held me tight.

'I-Is Nan O-OK?' I gulped out. But I already knew the answer.

'Cameron, she's dead,' Dad said as gently as he could. 'But she died peacefully, in her sleep.'

I cried and cried some more, while Dad rocked me without a word.

Chapter Twenty-Seven

See You Soon

Hello, Alex,

Yes, it's me! It's the New Year and I'm still standing – well, sitting, at any rate. I know it's gone but – Merry Christmas! And a very happy New Year! And it will be a happy New Year. D'you know why? Because the New Year will bring you. It's been a while since I've had the camcorder on to talk to you. A lot has happened. First and worst – Nan died a few weeks ago. I'm sorry to say it bluntly like that, but there is no other way to say it really, is there? Nan died in her sleep. Even now, I wonder if she knew something was going to happen. I keep replaying in my head all the things she said just before she died. I can't get over the feeling that it was as if she was saying goodbye. Is that silly? It probably is, but I've had a lot of time to think about it since. I shall miss her - desperately. I've never had anyone close to me die before. For a long while, I thought I'd never get over it. That doesn't mean I'm over it now, 'cos I'm not. Even now, it sort of makes me choke up. Nan was so full of life. I guess I'd convinced myself that everyone close to me was going to live for ever. Mum and Dad try to tell me that Nan had a good innings and it was just her time, but that doesn't really help. I didn't expect it to hurt inside quite so much. But it is getting better. I never thought that would happen either.

It's funny the way things work out, isn't it? My first transplant didn't take, so I had to decide whether or not I was going to have another one - a second transplant. Another pig's heart. To be honest, I wasn't going to, but a couple of days after Nan's death I decided that I would. I must be a glutton for punishment. The papers had a field day. Poor Dr Bryce has been called a butcher and there have been calls for him to be struck off and struck down and struck out and all sorts. I'm not supposed to know that, but one of the nurses told me.

You see, his second pig-heart patient died.

I didn't know her. I don't even know her name. All I know is that she was an artist and she was married with a son. I wonder how they're feeling now. No, I don't mean that. I know how they're feeling now, but I wonder if they still feel it was worth it. I guess they do. When you get right down to it, it's simple really. A chance of life against no chance at all. And although I didn't know her, I must admit that when I heard, it did upset me. I wonder what Trudy and the second pig − I think his name was Paul − would've made of all this. Wherever they are, they're probably laughing themselves stupid. But then again, maybe they're not. Spite and vindictiveness like that is more of a human thing than a pig thing - unless pigs really do think like the ones in Orwell's Animal Farm. I think I prefer the pigs that Dick King-Smith writes about, to be honest.

So why did I change my mind about the transplant? It had a lot to do with what Nan said to me on that last day, but I think it was mostly her dying. That sounds terrible, doesn't it? What I mean is, Nan's death made me realize that I was giving up too easily. I still have too many things to do and too many places to see and too many people to meet before I let go. I decided to have the operation for Mum and Dad and Nan, but mostly for myself.

But I'm not doing so well, this time around. It's taking me a long time to get my strength back. And I still get tired very easily. They only let me record this message because I promised to keep it short. I'm hoping to be around when you're born. I reckon that's do-able. If I'm not around, it won't be for want of trying. But whatever happens, Alex, just remember that I love you; I did from the time I knew about you.

You might hear things about me, things about this second operation and what happened before it and why I did it and such like – things that might upset you. So I'm going to tell you exactly what happened.

The papers are saying I tried to commit suicide by drowning myself in my local swimming pool. That's absolute rubbish. I didn't try to commit suicide. I wanted to touch the bottom of the pool and then I couldn't get back up to the surface, it's as simple as that. Some of the papers are trying to make out that I became so disgusted with the idea of having a pig's heart in my body that I wanted to bow out. But journalists will write any load of twaddle to try and sell their newspapers. So if someone tries to tell you that that's what happened, you tell them to go and play with the traffic or something.

Mum and Dad are outside waiting for me to finish. They're doing a lot better now. They're a lot calmer. And they're always kissing and cuddling. I think you did that, but I like to think that I had something to do with it as well. Perhaps, by watching me, they remembered how important, how precious every moment of every day is. D'you think I'm just full of myself? I probably am - but why not?! If I don't like me, then who else will?

I fancied Julie, but she went off me after my operation. She said I wasn't the same because my heart had changed. That upset me for a while. I think that played a big part in that pool business. I wanted to show her and Mum and Dad and mostly myself that I could do it. That not only was I the same, but I was better — not worse.

There's a lot of nonsense about me and Mum and Dad floating about at the moment. But if you want to know the truth, you ask one of us. Promise you'll do that. I can't wait to see you. I wish you were going to be born tomorrow. But then again, maybe I don't. You're the next challenge I've set myself. I know that doesn't make much sense to you — and it doesn't have to. Just know that I'm determined to hold you as soon as you're born. That's my new challenge and I like this one! It's a lot less strenuous than touching the bottom of my local swimming pool but a lot more work and much more uncertain. Still, it wouldn't be much of a challenge if it was easy, would it? When you're born in April, I'm going to hold you tight and say, 'Welcome to the world, Alex. I'm your big brother

Cameron Joshua Kelsey. And I hope one day you'll be as proud of me as I am of you.'

I'll see you soon, Alex.

This is Cameron Joshua Kelsey – signing off.

Malorie Blackman is acknowledged as one of today's most imaginative and convincing writers for young readers. *Noughts & Crosses* has won several prizes, including the Children's Book Award. Malorie is also the only author to have won the Young Telegraph/Gimme 5 Award twice with *Hacker* and *Thief!* Her work has appeared on screen, with *Pig-Heart Boy*, which was shortlisted for the Carnegie Medal, being adapted into a BAFTA-award-winning TV serial. Malorie has also written a number of titles for younger readers.

In 2005, Malorie was honoured with the Eleanor Farjeon Award in recognition of her distinguished contribution to the world of children's books.

In 2008, she received an OBE for her services to children's literature.

www.**malorieblackman**.co.uk

Reading Group